Sins, Lies & Spies

Black Brothers Series, Book Two

By Lisa Cardiff

Sins, Lies & Spies

Copyright © 2015 by Lisa Cardiff.
All rights reserved.
First Print Edition: February 2016

Limitless Publishing, LLC
Kailua, HI 96734
www.limitlesspublishing.com

Formatting: Limitless Publishing

ISBN-13: 978-1-68058-491-2
ISBN-10: 1-68058-491-X

PROLOGUE

Trinity

Age Ten...

Until last week, my life revolved around my mom. Her golden hair reminded me of the sun. When she smiled, her red lipstick was like a beacon drawing every gaze in the room. Her dark eyes managed to look both happy and sad at the same time, and I loved her more than anyone in the world. She was my world.

So when my mom walked out the front door of my uncle's house last Tuesday with a bright smile on her face promising our life was about to change for the better, I believed her. I believed we'd finally have a home of our own, and we wouldn't have to live with my grumpy uncle who grunted more than he spoke. I believed we'd have enough money for me to take all the dance lessons I could ever want. I believed she'd finally have more than a few minutes to spend with my sister, Faith, and me. Except she still hadn't returned.

"Staring at the window won't make her come home," my uncle grumbled, tossing a slice of pizza on the coffee table. Grease pooled on top of the cheese, making my stomach churn.

"She promised me," I mumbled, keeping my gaze glued out the window. I couldn't see anything except miles of inky darkness peppered with tiny pinpricks of light.

No headlights.

No lampposts.

No homes.

Even the moon couldn't be bothered to make an appearance tonight. My uncle lived in the middle of nowhere.

He drummed his beer bottle against his thigh. "Yeah, well, people lie. Get used to it."

I swiveled around and folded my arms across my chest. "My mom isn't a liar. She'll be back."

My uncle snorted, rubbing his hand down his reddish-blond beard. "Listen, Trinity. Your mother isn't coming back. You'll never see her again."

Tears snuck out of the corners of my eyes and my throat closed mid-inhalation. "But she gave me that music box and told me we'd have enough money to do whatever we wanted. She loves me. She loves Faith. She'd never leave us. We had plans."

"Honey," he sneered, tapping me in the middle of the forehead with his meaty index finger. I stumbled backward onto his stinky olive green couch. "The people you love the most will disappoint you the most. That's the way life works. Got it? By the way, that life lesson is free of charge."

"You're wrong. You don't know anything," I cried, shaking my head back and forth.

He twirled the hair under his chin into a sharp point until he resembled a comic book villain. "Believe what you want, but I don't want to hear any more talk about your mom." He aimed the mouth of his beer bottle at me. "Not one word. Not even her name. She's gone. The best thing we can do right now is pretend like she never existed. We'll be safer that way."

"I'll never forget my mom," I vowed between strangled sobs.

He stared at me pointedly. "Then you're a bigger fool than she was."

CHAPTER ONE

Knox

Present day…

"You look nice," a female voice murmured. "Where are you headed?"

Stifling a groan, I froze mid-step as I opened the front door of my apartment. "Brenna, what are you doing here?"

Her gaze darted to the side and she sucked her lower lip into her mouth. "You haven't returned my calls for over a week. I'm beginning to think you're avoiding me."

Beginning to think I'm avoiding her?

Pushing up the cuff of my shirt, I glanced at my watch. Ten minutes until the fundraiser at Representative Lang's house started. *Fuck!* I didn't have time for this.

"I never promised to call. In fact, I remember telling you on no less than four separate occasions that I'm not a relationship type of guy and not to get your expectations up."

Her mouth dropped open, and her bluish-green eyes narrowed. "Are you serious? After last weekend, I thought I meant something to—"

I clenched my teeth. "You've got to be kidding me," I grumbled under my breath. For the most part, I considered myself a patient man, but I couldn't deal with this shit right now. She knew the score. I never hid my intentions from her. I didn't play games. It wasn't my style. We discussed how I didn't want anything serious, and she assured me that she didn't either. Only, here we were. "Did I tell you that I changed my mind?"

She opened and closed her pouty, red lips. "No, but when I asked you if I could stay Saturday night, you agreed."

Casually buttoning the top button of my black tuxedo jacket, I stared at the oatmeal colored wall over her head. She was right. I should've known better, but I had worked my ass off all day and I was too tired to call her a cab. Give a woman a teaspoon of hope and she'd twist it into a white picket fence and two-point-five kids. I barely stifled the visible evidence of the shiver that ghosted down my spine.

I shoved my hands into my pockets, struggling to reel in my frustration. "I didn't have a choice. It was three in the morning, and we'd been drinking. If I'd thought you'd read anything into it, I would've called you a cab."

Her eyelashes fluttered, blinking away a few tears. "So that's it then?" She waved her hand back and forth between us. "You're not going to give us a chance?"

I glanced at my watch again. "No, like I told you when we met, I don't want a relationship. It doesn't matter if it's casual, committed or anything in between. My feelings haven't changed. My feelings will never change. If you wanted something more than an occasional hook-up, you have the wrong guy."

I wanted to tell her that the minute she showed up on my doorstep was the minute I decided I was done with her. Lately, I had toyed with the idea of wanting more than a casual fling, but tonight reminded me why I stayed true to my three-date rule. After date number three, women expected things. They started talking about feelings and hinting about a shared future. I was happy with my life. I didn't need a woman or a family. I wasn't cut out for that life.

At any rate, I didn't have the time or inclination to explain this to Brenna. The clock was ticking. I had a job to do and escalating this wouldn't help my cause. I was already cutting it close if I wanted to get in and out of Representative Lang's house without being caught.

"You're an asshole, Knox."

I refrained from rolling my eyes at the predictability of her comment. "I know. Are we finished, or do you want to continue arguing about why I need to change my mind about wanting a relationship just because you lied to me about not wanting one?" My voice trailed off as I pinned her with an icy glare.

Brenna's gaze shifted to the floor, then quickly down the narrow hallway. "Fuck you," she said without any heat. Her voice quivered and my chest squeezed with a tinge of guilt. I stifled the emotion as quickly as it materialized, and my anger surfaced again. I never lied to her.

Exhaling, I resisted the urge to respond with a crude comment. "Have a nice life, Brenna." I stepped around her and pushed open the door to the exit stairwell. I didn't want to call the elevator and risk prolonging my confrontation with her.

***

I stepped through the door of Representative Lang's home. The house hummed with polite conversation. Elegant people gathered in tiny circles, drinking champagne and martinis. Servers dressed in black pants and white collared shirts held silver trays with bite-sized appetizers.

I waved to acquaintances, and greeted anyone at the fundraiser who made eye contact. I feigned excitement for Lang's re-election campaign. I laughed at dumb jokes. I shook enough hands to consider making a quick detour to the bathroom. When that was done, I engaged him.

"Representative Lang." I clapped one hand on his left shoulder while I stuck out my other hand.

With steady eye contact, his fingers curled around mine in a practiced shake meant to demonstrate his authority. He was in his late fifties and at least four inches shorter than my six-foot-two frame. His watery blue eyes contrasted with his overly leathered skin. Gray hair liberally threaded the sides of his light brown hair. He looked like the typical politician, and I didn't mean that as a compliment.

"Mr. Black." He smiled a toothy, veneered grin that raised my hackles. "I'm surprised to see you here."

I tipped up my chin. "You know I couldn't pass up the chance to personally deliver my donation to your campaign." I pulled a folded check out of my pocket and handed it to him.

It disappeared into the pocket of his pants almost immediately. "Thank you. I appreciate your support. Do you know if Black Investments will be supporting my campaign this time around? There are rumblings of a new bill that will smother investment firms. I'd hate for your brother's company to get tangled up in miles of red tape."

My brother, Archer Black, ran an investment firm with billions of dollars in holdings. He recently relocated his headquarters to L.A. to support his fiancée's acting career. As much as I missed living near my brother, I couldn't be angry. He loved Langley, which was a fucking miracle. I never thought Archer would love anyone enough to get married. He was a cold bastard most of the time, but I couldn't fault him. Our childhood emotionally handicapped both of us in different ways. At least one of us managed to put the past behind us.

"I'll pass along the information to my brother. I'm sure he appreciates all your hard work. The country has a brighter future with you in office." I smiled like a jackass to conceal the lie. And no, lightning didn't strike me dead for the metaphorical pile of bullshit I heaped on his head.

A wide Cheshire cat grin split across his face. "Thanks for the vote of confidence."

"Anytime." I patted him on the shoulder again and excused myself. There was only so much smoke I could blow up someone's ass and still respect myself in the morning.

I grabbed a glass of champagne off a small round table near the back of the room and dashed down the white and black tiled hallway. According to my sources, Lang kept his personal computer in his home office at the rear of the house, adjacent to the bathroom.

Earlier today, I'd hacked into his home security system and dismantled the office and hallway cameras. Now, I had to pray no one wandered into the office in the ten minutes it'd take to access his computer, download everything from his hard drive onto a couple of thumb drives, and replace his USB cord.

As I walked into his office, I rapped lightly on the wood paneled wall. Even former military intelligence officers needed a bit of luck now and again.

I unplugged his computer, shoved the cord into my pocket, and replaced it with a special USB cord equipped with a tiny transceiver, which would communicate with my briefcase-sized field station set up in a vacant apartment my partner and I used as an office about four miles away. It would enable me to access data on Representative Lang's computer even if he disconnected it from the Internet as he frequently did.

Next, I inserted a thumb drive into the computer.

Tapping my finger against my thigh, I waited for the information to transfer until it was at capacity. "Hurry up," I mumbled as I glanced at the closed door across the room. When it finished, I double clicked on the folder for the thumb drive to verify the transfer, and I pulled it out, before quickly jamming another one into the USB slot.

The hardwood floor creaked behind me. The back of my neck prickled. Instinctively, I spun around, my hand flying to the gun hidden in the holster beneath my jacket.

A woman in a floor-length, gold strapless gown with a side slit to the middle of her thigh stood less than five feet from me. Her dark, nearly black hair draped over her shoulders in soft waves. Her lush lips were painted a deep red, and the lids of her chocolate eyes looked like she had sprinkled them with gold dust. Teardrop pearls dangled from her ears. She was one of the most beautiful women I'd ever seen. Unfortunately, she was also pointing a gun at me.

CHAPTER TWO

Trinity

Two creamy marble obelisks sat on either side of the entrance to Representative Lang's home office like sentries. A small metal lion head knocker was affixed to the center of the door, which didn't make sense in my opinion, but apparently, Lang liked drippy extravagance.

With a trembling hand, I clutched the tubular, bronze colored door handle and leaned my ear against the six-paneled, heavy wood door. I couldn't hear anything over steady hum of conversation and light tinkling of the piano from the party down the hall, but I knew he was in there. I saw him disappear down the hall with a glass of champagne in his hand when I arrived at Lang's party ten minutes ago. For the fifth time in as many minutes, I cursed my boss for causing me to arrive late. This was the first time he hadn't accompanied me on a mission. We role-played in preparation for tonight a hundred times, but it didn't make it any easier or less nerve-racking, especially now that I had to move to plan B.

I took one last deep breath to release my tension. It didn't help. If nerves conducted sound, mine would've been roaring like an airplane engine. Screw it, I couldn't back out now. Somehow over the past year, I'd become addicted to the rush of endorphins when I completed a mission.

I lived for it.

I got drunk on it.

Especially tonight, when I knew who I'd encounter on the other side of the door—Knox Black. He'd only been doing this for three or four years, but he and his partner were superstars. He had as close as someone in our line of work could get to a hundred percent success rate. Tonight he wouldn't be so lucky.

With disciplined precision, I pushed the lever down and opened the door, careful not to make a sound. The inside of the room tasted thick with anticipation.

One step.

Two steps.

Three steps…and the floorboard moaned underneath my feet. *Dammit!* So much for the element of surprise. Knox whirled around, and my breath caught. Either it was the tuxedo or he looked a hundred times better up close than in pictures.

His powerful muscles tensed, and something savage glinted inside his frosty, navy eyes. For one brief moment, my mission disappeared, and it was only Knox Black and me. My eyes lingered for a beat on the chiseled angles of his face, but just as quickly, I snapped out of my reverie and adjusted my gaze to his hand. My heart leaped as his hand inched inside his jacket, and he reached for what could only be a gun.

I pulled back the slide of my gun, and I heard the click of the ammunition as it moved into the chamber. "Don't even try it, Mr. Black."

He remained perfectly still, his hand tucked inside his tuxedo jacket for a tense second. Then he barked out a bitter laugh. "I seem to be at a disadvantage. You know my name, but I don't know yours."

"My name is not important."

"I beg to differ."

He smiled, but his face was taut and colorless, except for two flags of color high on the sharp blades of his cheekbones. His relaxed posture and feigned indifference didn't fool me. It'd only take one flicker of indecision from me, and he'd wrestle the gun out of my hand. Everything I heard about him suggested he had reflexes like quicksilver.

"I'm Trinity Jones." I smirked. "Maybe you've heard of me."

He hissed a curse under his breath, and the corners of his eyes crinkled. "Who's your client?"

"Tsk-tsk, Mr. Black. You know better than to ask me that question. You've been around long enough to know I can't reveal that information."

I tried to concentrate on his body language, but the edgy glint in his deep-set eyes and the twitch on the side of his jaw monopolized my attention.

"What do you want?" he asked, his voice deceptively serene, almost gentle.

"Give me the thumb drive sticking out of the computer, and then I want you to walk out of the office and leave the party."

"Ah." He shoved his hands into his pockets and shook his head. "And to think, I heard you were a competent and hardworking agent. You're every bit as lazy as the other hacks out there. You can't even do your own dirty work. Instead, you waited for me do the heavy lifting. Tell me. Are you afraid of hard work? Or are your skills that inferior?"

"I've always believed in the work smarter, not harder philosophy," I snapped, not hinting at my true intentions. He wanted the information, whereas I needed to destroy the thumb drives and the computer.

Knox leaned his hip against the desk, rubbing his hand along the square planes of his jaw. "At least you admit you're lazy. Most people wouldn't. Although I must say, I'm flattered by your confidence in my ability to extract the information from his computer."

"You're one of the best, or so I've been told. But that's not the issue right now." I jerked my gun toward the computer. "If you didn't notice, we don't exactly have time for a cordial meet and greet. Give me the thumb drive, before someone finds us in here."

He cocked one pale eyebrow as he snagged the memory stick out of the computer. "Now that would be interesting. How would you explain the gun?"

"I'm more than capable of thinking on my feet," I countered.

"I'm glad to hear that, Jones. I wouldn't want a

pretty woman like you to get in over your head."

The slightly husky rumble of my last name rolling from his lips sounded nice. Too nice. I didn't know exactly what was happening to me. For the first time in months, I was aware of another man—more aware than I should have been given the circumstance. Maybe I was finally over Miles, my mentor, and my boss. He screwed me over in more ways than I could count, but I hadn't dated anyone since. He took me under his wing when I had nothing and no one, and for that, I'd be forever grateful.

"Ah, it's touching you're concerned about me, but you shouldn't be. I haven't gotten this far on luck alone."

He crossed the room in a couple of giant strides and held out the thumb drive. A twinge of guilt twisted in my gut. I stared at the slim black drive for a second without reaching for it.

"Jones," Knox taunted, drawing out my last name. "Are you going to take this or are you wrestling with the ethics of stealing my work?"

Without dropping my gun, I grabbed it with my free hand, but he didn't release it. Locked in a silent battle, I heard Representative Lang's scratchy voice outside the office door. My head whipped to the side. *Dammit!* I hadn't fully closed the door.

What is wrong with me tonight? I'm not thinking clearly.

Knox closed the space between us, his face mere inches from mine and one side of his mouth hooked upward. A jolt of electricity arced between us. My blood felt like lava in my veins. He angled his head toward the cracked door. "An amateur mistake, don't you think?"

"Fuck you," I whispered, but I could hardly hear my words over the frantic swoosh of blood through my ears. My carefully crafted plans were going to blow up in my face. If I lowered my gun, Knox could take advantage of the moment and walk out of here with the memory stick. If I kept my gun aimed at Knox, I'd end up spending the night in jail, and I'd have to call Miles for bail money. I'd almost rather rot in prison than tell him I messed up. Sure, he was my boss, but that didn't mean I wanted to interact with him any more than absolutely necessary. Our relationship was dicey these days.

"I see your wheels spinning, but there's only one way we're going to get out of this now."

My dark eyes his clashed with his in a silent battle. "What do you have in mind?"

"We're going to put on a good show," he said, his warm breath tickling my face and sending shivers down my spine.

Electricity zigzagged through the air like a thunderstorm gathering strength on the edge of the horizon. My fingers involuntary twitched with the urge to sweep through his disheveled blond hair. He looked downright dreamy as his deep sapphire eyes zeroed in on my mouth. Before my mind registered his intent, he was kissing me. Like a puppet, I was too stunned to do anything except follow his direction. His tongue dueled with mine, and his arms circled my waist, pressing me firmly against his hard body, and I melted into him. Only our clothes and the cold metal of my gun separated us.

I heard a deep chuckle and murmured voices, but I couldn't bring myself to push Knox away. One of his hands edged around my neck, locking me in place and my ribcage squeezed tight around my heart. The kiss went on and on until I lost track of everything. He lit up every nerve ending in my body like a stick of dynamite nearing the end of its fuse. I never wanted it to end. I felt this kiss all the way down to my toes.

I was acutely aware of everything about him.

The spicy scent of his cologne.

The smooth weave of his jacket beneath my fingertips.

The faint fruity taste of champagne on his tongue.

The sound of a throat being cleared registered somewhere in the back of my mind. "I guess this room is taken."

Knox's lips lifted from mine, but he kept our bodies molded together. I gasped for breath.

He glanced to the side and quickly returned his attention to me. Apparently, the look on my face entertained him, because he flashed a wicked grin that made my heart stumble. "It's all yours, Representative Lang. We were just leaving."

In a too smooth move, he grazed his lips across mine one more time and snatched the gun out of my hand. With a quick flick of his wrist, he eased it inside of the waistband of his pants. He circled his arm around my hip. "Keep walking and put a smile on your face," he whispered in my ear, his warm breath sending a charged jolt down my spine.

Too stunned to think clearly, I did exactly as he asked. Heat rolled up my neck to my face. Damn my Irish blood.

"Sorry about that, Representative Lang," Knox said, a smirk on his face. "It won't happen again."

"Don't worry about it, Knox." Lang slapped his hand on Knox's shoulder as we passed him. "No harm was done. Don't forget to talk to your brother for me."

The minute we reached the foyer of Lang's home, he dropped his arm, and his eyes hardened, a fake smile ticking up the corners of his lips. "It was nice doing business with you, Jones. Maybe we'll run into each other again sometime."

Just like that, he was gone, the front door banging closed behind him. Shaken, I stared at the tiered crystal chandelier overhead for at least thirty seconds without moving, disappointment rolling in the pit of my stomach. I sucked in a gust of air, fighting the overwhelming urge to go after him and beg him to continue where we left off. All at once, the full impact of the last few minutes hit me like a punch to the gut. Knox left with my gun and the memory stick.

"Asshole," I muttered.

CHAPTER THREE

Knox

"How'd it go?" Jack swiveled around in his chair when I opened the door to our office, his eyebrows raised expectantly. Like every other day, he looked perpetually rumpled.

Jack and I started a private military company specializing in intelligence-gathering the day we finished our tour of duty. While we both loved working as Naval Intelligence officers, neither of us liked the constraints placed on us in the public sector. We thought we could do more as private contractors. Business was slow for the first year, and I'd accepted a part-time computer security gig with my brother at Black Investments to pay our bills. Fortunately, for the last three or four years, we had more work than we could comfortably handle. In fact, we regularly turned away jobs. I'd have more time if I stopped working for Archer, but it kept us in regular contact after he moved to L.A.

"I got what we needed and replaced the USB

cord, but it wasn't as seamless as I would've liked." I slipped off my tuxedo jacket and slung it over the back of my black leather chair.

Jack leaned forward, bracing his elbows on his knees. "What the hell happened? You do know what's at risk here, right?"

"Relax, Jack," I said, settling into the desk chair and opening my laptop. I tossed the thumb drives on the desk. Instead of having a traditional office, Jack and I opted to set up shop in a large industrial studio apartment that functioned as a war room of sorts. This way we didn't waste time going back and forth and sending emails filled with information better communicated without a digital record. "Like I said, we got what we wanted."

"Then why did you come back here tonight instead of going home?" Jack asked.

"Because I knew your pathetic ass would still be here." Jack crashed on the pullout sofa seven out of ten nights. At first, I admired his dedication, but now I saw it for what it was—an avoidance technique. He married his girlfriend of three months in Las Vegas the day before he had to report for duty. Since he got out of the service, they spent more time fighting than anything else. I didn't understand why he refused to call it quits. They didn't have kids, and they didn't have many joint assets. Every time I brought up the topic, he shut me down faster than a virgin on prom night, so I stopped asking about her and the marriage years ago. I followed his lead and pretended as though she didn't exist.

"So what happened tonight?"

I stretched out my legs in front of me and crossed my ankles. "Trinity Jones popped into Lang's office just as I finished transferring the information to the last thumb drive."

Jack leaned back and ruffled his fingers through his brown hair. "Tell me you're kidding."

I blew out a long breath. "If only that were true."

He crossed his ankle over the opposite knee, and tipped his head toward the ceiling, all while tapping his pen against the edge of the table. "Fuuuck." He slapped his hand against the armrest of his chair. "Miles Knightly trained her. She. Works. With. *Him.*"

I groaned. "Fucking hell."

To put it mildly, Miles and I didn't see eye to eye. We bumped heads more than once since Jack and I started freelancing. He was a world-class asshole who lacked morals. Granted, in this line of work morals were pliable and lines were blurred, but unlike Miles, I only accepted cases on the right side of the law or what I perceived to be the right side of the law. In this current matter, he was on the wrong side. I just needed the evidence to back up my suspicions.

I rubbed my hand along the side of my face. "Miles has been one step ahead of us this whole investigation. He knows our next move before we do, and I'm damn sick of it."

"Yeah, but you walked away with the thumb drives, not her. If our luck holds, we'll have everything we need to uncover all the parties involved in this blackmail scheme by the end of the week."

"Let's hope so." I drummed my fingers on my thigh. "I'll question Trinity and see if I can get any information out of her."

"Hm." Jack's eyebrows jumped up his forehead. "That's interesting."

My eyes narrowed. "What's that supposed to mean?"

He shrugged, a smile tugging at the corners of his lips. "I've seen Trinity Jones a time or two."

"So what?"

His smile widened. "Well, she's not exactly hard on the eyes."

I scanned through the subject lines of the emails piling up in my inbox. "Yeah, well, I didn't notice. I was too focused on the gun she aimed at my head."

"Uh-huh." Jack chuckled softly. "It's kind of hard to overlook a five-foot-ten brunette who looks like a swimsuit model, but if that's what you're telling yourself, I'll go along with it. Just be careful. She's not some woman you can toy with for a couple of weeks and show the door."

Ignoring his comment, I searched for any correspondence requiring my immediate attention. When I didn't see anything, I slammed the laptop closed again. "I'm outta here. I have an early meeting at the Black Investments' satellite office, so I'll catch up with you tomorrow afternoon." I shoved the laptop into my briefcase, stood up and snagged my jacket off the back of my chair. I made it all the way to the door before Jack said anything.

"I'm not lecturing you. I just want you to proceed with caution where Trinity Jones is concerned. She's not like the other women who come and go in your life. She works in the same field as you, and the last thing we need is a new enemy because you didn't keep it in your pants."

I paused, one hand gripping the doorknob. "Don't treat me like a child." I whirled around to face him. "I know exactly what's at stake, but rest assured, I'm only interested in what she can tell me about Representative Lang and his connection to Miles Knightly."

To some extent, I told the truth. I couldn't get involved with Trinity Jones. My brain knew that, but from the minute I saw her pointing that gun at me, I wanted to taste her. Touch her. Kiss her. Despite my better judgment, I did exactly that when Lang's sudden appearance gave me the opening I needed.

Jack stared at me, a hesitant frown on his face, then nodded. "Okay, I believe you." He slid his fingers along his lips, and I thought he was finished lecturing me for the night. Unfortunately, he wasn't.

"Trinity Jones is more than Miles Knightly's pet project. They were involved intimately for at least a year; maybe longer. I don't know the details. She still collaborates with him, but the relationship ended when she discovered Miles never firmly severed ties with his ex-wife."

"Why are you telling me this?"

"Because Miles still considers her his property, and if something happened between you two or if you want to pursue her—"

I raised my hand, interrupting him. "Nothing happened and even if it did, you've known me long enough to realize I never get hung up on any woman," I said, forcing my voice to remain even and relaxed. Regrettably, jealousy and anger teemed beneath the surface. I could deal with the anger. Anger management shaped my entire childhood, but I didn't do the jealous thing. With the exception of my brothers, I never cared about anyone or anything enough to inspire that emotion.

"There's always an exception to every *never*. One day a woman will come along who will change your mind and knock you on your ass." Jack chuckled. "I just hope I get a front row seat to the whole thing."

A burst of laughter escaped my mouth. "Yeah, you and every woman I've ever dated. But trust me, Trinity Jones isn't that woman."

CHAPTER FOUR

Trinity

I hated D.C. in the winter. The trees were grayish sticks. The low-hanging clouds muddied the sky. The cold, wet air seeped into my bones like I wasn't wearing a stitch of clothing. My skirt didn't help matters. I flipped up the collar of my black trench coat and folded my arms across my body. Some days, I felt like I'd never get warm again.

As much as I loathed admitting it, days like this made me miss the mild winters of Texas. I got the hell out of there days after I turned twenty-one and I hadn't been back, but it didn't mean I wanted to spend the rest of my life in D.C. I never intended to live here more than a year, but a year turned into two. Then, I met Miles. He took me under his wing a year and a half ago. First I filed papers for him in his home office, but it quickly turned into more. He mentored me and gave me a career and new life.

For the most part, we had a good working relationship. I liked him, and I admired how hard he worked. As the months progressed, forty hours a week turned into sixty, then ninety. On particularly late nights, I slept in his guest room. One night he kissed me, and somehow we ended up in a relationship. Days bled into months. I thought we were in love and on the road to getting married. Apparently, he didn't agree. Despite our disastrous ending, I'd continued working with him after he screwed me over. I needed the money for my sister.

I opened the door to Miles's house with the key he gave me when we started dating. He never asked for it back, and I never offered. I didn't want to deal with the permanency of the gesture. Creeping down the hallway, I paused a few times to listen for voices coming from his office. I wished I could avoid this confrontation for another day until I came up with a solid plan to recover the thumb drives from Knox and get into Lang's house and destroy his computer. He rarely, if ever, connected the computer to the internet, which ruled out hacking as a viable alternative. Besides breaking into Knox's home and office and stealing the thumb drives and destroying any copies, I didn't have any promising ideas. I wasn't looking forward to another confrontation with him either. He unsettled me.

"Nice of you to finally show your face," Miles growled, his gravely voice putting me on edge.

I sent him a brief text last night telling him I hadn't succeeded and avoided him as long as possible. I wanted to give him time to calm down before we met in person. When his phone calls and text messages escalated to the point of harassment this afternoon, I caved and drove to his house after dinner.

I rested my hip against the corner of his desk. "I've been busy."

"Busy avoiding me," he said. His heated, dark eyes swept over my body. I used to like that look. Now it pissed me off. I curled my hands around the square edge of the desk, just barely resisting the urge to yank on the hem of my skirt. He lost the right to look at me as anything other than a colleague the minute he started screwing his ex-wife on the side while we were together. "You look beautiful as always, Trinity," he said, his words almost reverent.

I barely checked the urge to roll my eyes. His compliments were meaningless. "I've been working on alternatives to recover the information Knox Black lifted from Lang's private computer."

He chewed on the end of his pen, his eyes never leaving mine. "Have you come up with anything?"

I rubbed my hand down my neck. "I have some ideas, but nothing definitive at this point."

"Now that Knox has the information, we're on borrowed time. We need to destroy it before he realizes what he has. Otherwise this whole thing will explode in my face."

I nodded. "I'm working on it. Give me a couple more days."

"We don't have a couple of days. My client isn't going to like this." He tossed his pen on top of the desk. "Hell, I don't like this."

"I know, but unless I shot Knox in front of Representative Lang, it couldn't be avoided." My shoulders sagged in defeat, but I quickly rolled them back again. I couldn't show any weakness around Miles. He was like a shark smelling blood. "Besides, none of this would've happened if you hadn't waylaid me on the way to the party," I said, trying to turn the tables.

When I walked out my front door last night to leave for Lang's house, Miles was waiting for me. He wanted to give me a ride to the party to talk about us. Like so many times over the last month, we exchanged barbs, and I ended up being late.

He leaned back in his chair and propped his hands behind his head. "You knew Knox Black getting to the computer first was a possibility. It shouldn't have mattered. We had a backup plan. Why didn't you stick to it?"

Stalling, I picked up the snow globe on his desk and shook it. Apparently, he bought it for his fourteen-year-old daughter last Christmas, but she didn't want it. Somehow, it found a permanent home on his desk, collecting dust. Part of me wanted to look him in the eye and come clean about everything, and apologize for being distracted by a stupid, meaningless kiss, but I knew a confession would only prolong this interrogation. I didn't want to spend any more time in Miles's company than absolutely necessary. He knew how to manipulate me and make me want stupid things—like him.

"I managed to get the thumb drive from Knox Black, but then Lang walked in the office. Knox diverted my attention and stole the thumb drive from me."

He stood up, closed the distance between us, and chucked me under the chin with two fingers. "And you just let him take it? That doesn't sound like you. What am I missing here?"

My pulse racing, I smacked his hand away from my face. "Nothing. Your plan was flawed. I needed to upload the virus before Knox Black got to the computer. There were too many people at the party. I couldn't do anything to stop him, and he knew it. He didn't take me seriously."

He pursed his lips. "What's that supposed to mean?"

I pushed away from the desk and smoothed the folds of my skirt. "Nothing. I need to take off. I'll be in touch tomorrow."

"We need to destroy the information from Lang's computer. Conceding is not an option." Looking down, he rubbed his temples. "My client will go nuclear if we fail."

My brows pinched together. "Nobody likes failure, but sometimes it happens. We need a contingency plan for what to do next."

"There is no next. We need to stop that motherfucker before he ruins everything," he growled heatedly.

"I don't get it. Why does the client want to get rid of those files, anyway? What's so important about them?"

He yanked on his already loosened tie and glanced to the side. "I don't know exactly, and I don't care. Those were his instructions, and he's not someone to fuck with. He'll stick a knife in my throat before I finish explaining why we failed. He's not like the other people I've worked for. He's ruthless, Trinity, and I don't say that lightly. I've worked with some bad people in my life, but he's in a league of his own." He blew out a breath. "That's all I'm going to say about it. You don't need to know anything else."

A tremor zipped down my spine and my muscles stiffened. I inhaled through my nose and rolled back my shoulders. Probing him for information he didn't want to share was a waste of energy, and a small part of me didn't want to know anything else. "I'll see what I can do. See you tomorrow."

"Wait. Do you want to stay for dinner?" He tugged on the end of my ponytail, an expectant smile on his face. "I ordered Chinese. Your favorite. It should be here any minute."

I focused on the black and white landscape photos hanging on the wall behind his desk. "I already ate."

He stepped closer to me, the front of his pants brushing the side of my thigh. "Don't make me eat alone. We haven't spent any quality time together in a while. I miss you." He lowered his voice, his lips only inches from my ear. "I miss us. We were good together. Don't you think it's time we worked this out? Every time we get close, you push me away again."

My face flamed with humiliation as memories of what happened between us a week after we broke up taunted me. We'd been working late. In a moment of weakness, he kissed me and one thing led to another. The next day and every day afterward, I rationalized the whole thing as me being lonely and nostalgic for what I thought we had before the truth slapped me across the face.

Marrying him and building a life together had been the next step in my life for almost a year, and I didn't have a contingency plan. Part of me wanted to give in and try again even though I knew this back and forth between us had to stop. It was unhealthy.

"Miles." I held up one hand as I took a few steps backward to put space between us. "I don't want to keep going in circles. We're over, and nothing you do will change my mind. If you can't keep this professional, we need to cut ties."

"You didn't object a couple of weeks ago," he said, his voice hard, cold; and I shivered. Two steps forward and he loomed over me. His jaw was set, and his dark eyes glittered.

I shook my head. "I made a mistake. I'm sorry if I gave you the impression I wanted to reconcile. That was never my intention because it couldn't be further from the truth. I can't do this again."

His mouth opened, but just as quickly hinged closed, his eyes narrowing almost imperceptibly. "I've apologized for what happened countless times. Too many times. You need to start acting like an adult instead of a petulant child, punishing me for a few missteps." He scraped his fingers down his neck. "You've given me more mixed signals than a drunken music conductor."

"A few missteps?" I scoffed, my hands trembling and anger heating my skin. "You were sleeping with your ex-wife. She thought the two of you had reconciled. We were shopping for engagement rings. I thought we were getting married. You were stringing us both along." I bit down on my lower lip, restraining the urge to spit dozens of sarcastic insults. I didn't want to back him into a corner and force him to sever our working relationship. I had enough upheaval in my life right now. I needed stability so I could keep helping my sister. She deserved everything I could give her and more.

"I know. I know." He raised his hands in surrender. "I shouldn't have touched her. I realize that, but we have a complicated history. I know it's not an excuse, but one thing led to another and I fell into an old habit. It's all over now. She understands that, and it won't happen again. I promise."

"You're right." I paused for a beat, summoning the backbone to push him away. "It won't because I've moved on."

His eyebrows slanted downward. "Are you seeing someone?"

"Yes," I lied. "I'm late. I need to go."

"Wait." He grabbed my wrist. "Who is he?"

"No one you know. We've only gone out once, but I like him."

"It'll never work. He won't understand what you do, why you spend time with me, or why you have irregular hours."

"Maybe. Maybe not, but it isn't your business." I pried his hands off my wrist and shrugged. "By the way, you don't have the right to touch me anymore."

"Don't I?" he said, his hand stroking the side of my face. My breath stalled inside of my lungs for a moment, then gusted out in one giant whoosh.

"No." Our eyes locked in a wordless struggle. "You had your chance. I'm doing what I should have done months ago. I'm moving on."

"Listen, Tri." He lowered his voice an octave, clasping his hands around the swells of my hips. "Give me one more chance. I sorted everything out with my ex. She won't be an issue. I want to make this work. She's my past. You're my future. Let me know how I can make this up to you."

I rubbed a hand down the side of my face as I stepped out of his hold. "I don't know. I don't think I can go there yet. I'm not ready."

"Can you try? We don't have to rush anything. Just keep an open mind."

I swallowed hard. I shouldn't trust him, but a tiny dysfunctional part of me wanted to pretend the last few months hadn't happened and be happy again. For a small moment in time, I was on the cusp of getting engaged and living happily ever after. Since I was little, I'd dreamed of having the perfect someone in my life who'd never disappointment me or abandon me.

I pulled my lower lip between my teeth, studying him before I answered. "I'm not going to promise anything, but I'll keep an open mind about our future."

"That's a start." He pressed a kiss to the corner of my mouth and a flicker of self-hatred shot through my veins. "You won't regret this. I promise."

Why can't I believe him? Trust him? Damn him. Damn me.

Acid rolled in my stomach at the thought of letting Miles into my life again. I couldn't stop the nagging feeling he'd hurt me again.

"I'll be in touch tomorrow," I said, stepping out of his office.

***

I cased the entire length of the block of Knox's three-story apartment building. Interior lights winked at me, taunting me with their warmth. The night clung to the buildings as I darted in and out of the shadows, testing whether or not anyone had spotted me. An occasional car drove by, its lights reflecting off the wet pavement. No one had walked by in the last thirty minutes. Pausing at the side entrance of his building, I propped my back against the wall. The icy brick bit into my back, but I ignored it, my attention focused on the yellow glow of lights shining through the corner window on the third floor. Knox was in his bedroom and awake unless he slept with his lights on. I eyed the windows below his. Most were dark and quiet.

"Go to bed, already," I hissed under my breath.

I promised myself I'd leave if he didn't turn off his light in the next fifteen minutes. Any longer, and I might freeze. My teeth chattered nonstop. My legs felt like twin popsicles and my feet resembled lumps of ice. I should've gone home and changed into more appropriate clothes, but I didn't want Miles to discover I lied to him about having plans.

As if fate knew I couldn't wait any longer, the light in Knox's room turned off and the window blurred into the darkness. Fear and excitement pumped fast through my veins like a drug. I pushed away from the wall and pulled a slim bag of tools from my pocket. Growing up with an uncle who stole cars in his late teenage years came in handy, especially when I needed to pick locks.

CHAPTER FIVE

Knox

My eyes popped open. Moonlight shimmered through the cracks of my drapes. Wide awake, I reached for the gun hidden in the sideboard of my bed. As quietly as possible, I rolled off the mattress and waited. Most people would've attributed the sounds to an overactive imagination, but I didn't think so. Every nerve in my body howled in warning. Somebody was inside my apartment.

The light echo of leather shoes clapped against my hardwood floors. The rustle of papers shuffling drifted through the air. If I strained hard enough, I heard the soft puffs of someone breathing.

Stepping out of my bedroom, I inched around the corner and paused, using the shadows as a cloak as I listened. The noises came from the guest bedroom I used as a personal office. With my back pressing into the wall and my gun in front of me, I crept down the hall. When I reached the entrance, I peeked into the room and froze.

Trinity Jones crouched in front of my filing cabinet with her back to me, a slim metal tool hanging out of her pocket. Her long dark hair was in a ponytail that brushed the middle of her upper back with every movement. Her dark colored skirt clung to her ass and thighs, leaving nothing to the imagination. I blew out a breath. I didn't want to deal with this shit tonight. I went to bed late too late for my scheduled early morning meeting.

"To what do I owe this pleasure?"

In one smooth motion, she jumped to her feet and whirled around. Mascara smudged the skin beneath her eyes, but other than that, she looked fresh. Beautiful. "You tricked me. You didn't give me what I asked for."

I laughed. "I never intended to give it to you. I just let you believe I would for a few minutes."

She rolled her eyes and stepped around my desk. "And that's why I'm here. I need those thumb drives and any copies."

"And you thought you'd find it sitting around in my home office?"

She shrugged. "It was worth a try."

I lowered my gun and took a few cautious steps forward. I didn't have any illusions that Trinity wasn't armed or trained in martial arts. Miles might be an asshole, but he did a respectable job of grooming the people who worked for him.

"Well, they're not here. In fact, they're long gone. I passed them along last night." It was a lie; Jack and I were still combing over every last document, video, picture, and photograph lifted from Lang's computer. Once that was done, I'd handle the case myself. Sometimes politics trumped evidence, and the Department of Justice refused to prosecute the offenders. I didn't like it, but that was exactly what would happen with Lang. All the evidence pointed to treason and blackmail, but the Administration didn't care. They considered a conviction more of a liability than letting the guilty walk away with a slap on the hand.

She chewed on her lower lip. "You're lying."

"No. I'm not." I smirked. "So be a good girl and run along before this encounter becomes even more unpleasant."

She curled her hands into fists, her coffee colored eyes glittering. "Don't threaten me."

I pointed toward the door. "You're in my home. I'm entitled to do whatever I want."

She stared at me for a prolonged beat, her gaze tracing the lines of my naked torso, before focusing on my face. "Fine. I'll leave."

She took a few steps in the direction of the door to my office, and I noticed the bulge inside her jacket. I grabbed her wrist as her body came even with mine. Her bones were startlingly tiny. My finger and thumb easily overlapped the circumference.

"Did you find anything interesting?" I asked, my tone deceptively pleasant.

Her hair whipped around her chin as she turned to face me. She twisted her wrist, but I didn't release her. "Not particularly."

I pinned her with my stare. "Great. Then you won't mind me taking this from you." My hand shot inside her jacket and I pulled out a couple of files.

I flipped through the labels.

Benton Family.

Representative Lang.

Amy Black.

She stole the file on my mom.

My entire childhood, I had a recurring daydream of my father banging on the front door of our shitty trailer in that even shittier town in Arizona and demanding to take me away from there. By the time I reached thirteen, I gave up hope, and I focused on getting the hell out of there and away from my mom.

Last year, I spent some time investigating my mother's relationships around the time I was born. My mom told me more times than I could count that she didn't remember anything about my father. She claimed she had a drunken one-night stand and ended up pregnant, but I didn't believe her, and my research backed up my instincts. My mom may have spent a good chunk of my formative years working as a high-paid escort of sorts, but she had a very short list of steady clients. I had narrowed the list to two men who could be my father.

Between Archer's quest for revenge against Senator Wharton and the explosion of business at my security and intelligence firm, I didn't have the time to dig any deeper and part of me didn't want to know anyway. Somehow over the past year, it no longer mattered who fathered me, but it didn't mean I liked Trinity prying into my personal business.

As I stared at the label on the inch-thick file folder, I felt the familiar sensation of a hundred pound weight on my back, my mind drunk on unwanted memories. I had forgotten, or maybe just hadn't wanted to recall, the feeling of dejection and hopelessness of growing up poor and without anyone who cared about me except my brother Archer.

"You're spying on me. Is this late night visit another errand for your piece of shit boyfriend? Tell me. Why does he make you do all his dirty work?" Hate coated my words, but it wasn't directed at her. Not really.

Her eyes narrowed and she yanked her hand away from me. I didn't resist. I needed her to get out of my home before I snapped. I couldn't stand the thought of people prying into my personal business. I didn't share my history with anyone. Sure, I disclosed a rose-colored version of my history to the government to get security clearance, but nobody except Archer and his fiancée knew the real truth. The real truth was so much uglier than I wanted to reveal.

The corners of her lips turned down. "My boyfriend?"

"Yes. I'm talking about Miles." I folded my arms across my chest. "By the way, you have poor taste in men."

"Miles isn't my boyfriend. He's a business associate." The melancholy in her voice hit me like a punch to the gut.

"Oh really? That's not what I heard."

She rocked back on her heels and laughed, but it

wasn't genuine. "Yeah, well, your sources are wrong."

Our eyes met, and I took the opportunity to study her face. I could get lost in those eyes. They were dark and endless. My attention dipped to her mouth. Even pursed in anger, it looked good enough to nibble on.

Beneath her sharp tongue and thick armor, I sensed uncertainty and loneliness. For a fleeting second, I wanted to delve into the layers that made Trinity Jones tick. I shook my head. What the hell was I doing waxing poetic about some woman who broke into my home and searched my personal and work files?

"Why did you take these files?" I yelled, angrier with myself now than with her.

She flinched, but immediately shrugged nonchalantly, trying to cover her reaction. "They looked interesting."

"You're lying."

"So what? What are you going to do about it?"

The muscle in my jaw twitched from clenching my teeth. "Stay away from me, Jones. The trick you pulled at Representative Lang's home was business and I'll let it go for now. But if I find out you or Miles are meddling in my private matters, I won't hesitate to destroy both of you."

Warning delivered, I walked to my front door, not bothering to turn around to see if she was following me. I flung open the door. She took a few steps, her shoes clicking against the floor, before pausing at the threshold.

She stared at me, assessing me, trying to read my

thoughts. "This isn't over. Not by a long shot."

"Yes, and that's what separates the good agents from the bad agents."

"And what's that exactly?"

"The intelligent ones recognize when they've been beaten and they cut their losses and move on. The dumb ones just keep spinning their wheels, wasting more time and resources all to come to the same conclusion."

She leaned forward, and she was so close to me. The tip of her pink tongue darted out of her mouth. Awareness swirled through the air, and invisible arrows prickled my suddenly feverish skin. Dammit, I had the urge to kiss her again. I doubted she'd appreciate the gesture, especially after I just finished insulting her intellect.

Instead, I twisted a silky strand of her hair around my finger, my gaze glued to the contrast between my skin and her inky mane.

Dark and light.

Night and Day.

Yin and yang.

Mixed messages swirled in the air, making it heavy. She froze, her eyes wide with shock and something elusive.

Desire?

Anger?

Interest?

Compassion?

Incapable of stopping myself, I slanted forward, halving the space between us. I could hear the chaotic drum of her heart. She smelled citrusy— almost like a lemon meringue pie—and I had the ridiculous urge to lick the long column of her throat. Her breath caught and her lips parted, a faint blush moving up her cheeks. Time suspended, shimmering around us with unleashed potential. A hundred thoughts trickled through my mind, sending a dark, unsettling heat rippling through my body. If I were a gambling man, I would've bet she wanted me to kiss her and a whole lot more. I felt like I was losing my mind because there was no way anything could happen between us.

Her warm chocolate eyes hardened, turning black, and all too soon, she snapped out of whatever trance we were under. She slapped my hand away. "I'm not afraid of you, Knox Black." The smoky warmth of her voice made my heart bang against my ribcage.

She turned on her heel, slamming the door behind her. And then, she was gone, leaving a whirl of citrus perfume and still unanswered questions in her wake. Dumbfounded, I stared at the closed door wondering what in the hell just happened and why I let Trinity Jones walk out of here without interrogating her.

CHAPTER SIX

Trinity

Loud music filled the bar where I used to work as a bartender. I recognized some of the faces of long time customers, and I waved to a few of my former coworkers as my heels clicked over the worn wide planked floor. People were packed wall-to-wall in the narrow space, slamming back beers and other concoctions. Excited, boisterous and carefree voices rang out, celebrating the beginning of a new weekend.

I plopped down on the barstool across from my best friend, Leslie. She owned the bar where I found my first job after I moved to D.C. I showed up for a job interview, and she hired me on the spot.

Originally, I had planned to work nights and attend community college during the day. It never happened. I never had enough money to spare. Between rent and other meager living expenses, I couldn't save more than a hundred or so dollars a month. Every time I got close to having enough money for a class or two, some event would derail everything, and I'd have to start all over again.

"I didn't think you'd show," Leslie said as she slid a drink across the translucent, backlit onyx counter.

"Yeah, yeah. I'm running later than I expected." I lifted the cup to my lips and frowned when the warm, smoky liquid splashed onto my tongue. When we were dating, Miles's habit of ordering bourbon neat rubbed off on me. At the time, I thought it was sophisticated, but now I acknowledged the truth. I hated the taste of whiskey. I was a vodka girl. I gulped it down anyway, craving the relaxation found at the bottom of a few drinks.

She sucked her lips into her mouth. "What happened?"

I glanced to the side, taking in the drunken people walking in jagged lines. "I had a shitty night and even shittier day. I need a drink or five." I fought to keep the smirk off my face. My explanation had to be the understatement of the century.

She shifted forward, bracing her pointy elbows on the smooth countertop. Leslie was my complete opposite. She resembled a dainty little elf with light blonde, almost white hair and fine facial features.

"What happened?"

I groaned, slumping in my seat. "I had some stuff to take care of for Miles." I never shared what kind of work I did. I couldn't. Unfortunately, the confrontation with Knox Black last night paled in comparison to what happened today. When I told

Miles that Knox had already handed the thumb drives over to his client, he fucking lost his mind. He screamed. He broke things. He threw his files off his desk.

Her sky blue eyes narrowed. "Why are you still working for him?"

"The money—"

She held up her hand. "Don't lie to me. You don't need the money. Not like when you showed up for an interview at the bar three years ago. You were desperate, but you're not anymore."

"I'm not doing it for me. I'm doing it for Faith. She needs me. I promised her I'd help her any way I could." I may have left my sister in the care of my inattentive uncle when I moved, but I never forgot about her. I sent her money every month starting the day I received my first paycheck. Now, I paid her college tuition. I wanted her to have opportunities I never had. I owed her that. I wouldn't be like my mom and abandon my family. Family first. Since the day my mom left, I lived by that mantra. Even if they didn't want it, all of my family members had my unconditional loyalty.

She raised her eyebrows. "Faith can get a loan like thousands of other college kids. It won't kill her, and you'll find something else soon enough. You've already wasted too many years of your life on him. You need to get the hell away from him while you're still able. He's not going to give up on you."

I looked down, the tips of my ears burning. She was referencing my hook-up with Miles a couple of weeks ago. I shouldn't have breathed a word about it, but I was an emotional mess after it happened. I felt like I had betrayed her and myself, and in a moment of weakness I confessed everything. In retrospect, it wasn't the best idea. She never let a single opportunity slip to note her disapproval of my continued relationship with him, even though it had been strictly professional for the past few weeks. She'd lose it if she knew I promised him I'd think about giving him another chance.

"I know. I'm going to start looking for something else soon. I've put out some feelers. It won't be long now." The truth was, I hadn't done a damn thing. The fear of Miles finding out I was looking for a new job paralyzed me.

In a matter of days, I probably wouldn't have an alternative. Normally, Miles approached our missions with a cool efficiency that I admired, but today he was crazed. I walked out of his office, mid-tantrum, and sent every one of his calls to voicemail since then. Something about the information on Representative Lang's personal computer had him on edge. In fact, Miles had been acting weird for months. Every time I pushed for answers, he deflected all of my questions.

"Good." She patted me on the arm. "I'd hate for you to waste any more time on that asshole."

Smiling faintly, I tapped the side of my glass. "So I found some new information about my mom."

Her eyes widened. "What? How?"

I shifted in my seat. "I came across her name on a file while I was doing some research for Miles. I didn't get the chance to read it, but who knows?" I shrugged. "This might be the break I've been looking for."

"What are you going to do?"

I chuckled. "Try to get my hands on that file again and make a copy."

"Is it at Miles's office?"

I chewed on the inside of my lower lip. "Not exactly."

She studied me curiously, her lips stretched into a pinched line. "Do I even want to ask?"

"No. Please don't."

She shook her head, and her short hair danced around her face like a puff of cotton. "You haven't told me much about what you do for Miles, but I put together enough bits and pieces of information to know it's not exactly risk-free." She sighed. "Be careful, okay? Don't put yourself in any more danger to dig up dirt on your mom. Some things are better left in the past. Maybe your mom falls into that category. If she wanted to be part of your life, she would've made it happen, or at least contacted you."

I couldn't respond because, at this point, I refused to stop looking. I needed to know what happened to my mother. After spending the first years of my life drifting from place to place, my mom settled down in a small town. It didn't last long. She ended up pregnant with Faith, and we moved in with my uncle.

Not too long after Faith was born, my mom didn't come home from work one night. I spent an entire week glued to our front window crying and waiting for her to return until one day my uncle couldn't take it anymore. He told me she'd never come back. He was right. I never heard a word from her again, and my uncle refused to talk about her. Every lead I had on her was a dead end…until now. Knox Black held the key. I was certain of it.

Impatiently, I bounced my leg up and down. "We'll see. I haven't decided what, if anything, I'm going to do with the information," I finally answered.

Staring over at me, she wiped the counter with a damp towel, silently absorbing my words. "Okay. Just think before you jump."

"Hey, Les," a guy I vaguely recognized shouted from the end of the bar. "Can I get a refill?" He raised his empty glass, waving it back and forth.

"I'm on it," she said before turning her attention back to me. "Are you stickin' around for a while? I'm off in an hour if you want to grab something to eat."

Twirling a paper coaster in circles, I shook my head. "I don't think so. I'm dead on my feet."

She lifted the bottle of caramel-colored whiskey and leaned over the bar. I slapped my hand over the top of my glass. "I'll have vodka on the rocks this time."

Relief washed over her face, and she smirked. "About fucking time, Trinity. I was wondering when you'd start being yourself again instead embracing the persona Miles created." She squeezed my hand. "Don't let anyone make you feel less than you are. You've lived through some crappy stuff, but you made it through without becoming a hard person. You should wear your life experiences as a badge of honor instead of a black mark."

I crossed then uncrossed my legs, letting her words sink in. "I know. I got lost for a while, but I'm my own person. I won't get wrapped up in anyone else ever again." I couldn't. I had to stay focused so I could help Faith. Even if I worked things out with Miles, it'd be different this time. I wouldn't lose my identity. I wouldn't blindly follow him or believe him. I'd keep my eyes open.

Genuine relief washed over her face, and she knocked her knuckles against the counter two times. "Let's hope so."

CHAPTER SEVEN

Knox

From the living room of Trinity Jones's townhome, I heard keys jingle outside the door. The deadbolt clicked and the heavy paneled door pushed open.

About freaking time.

"Jesus, Knox." Trinity froze mid-step with her hand over her heart. "What are you doing here?"

Leaning back in the chair, I propped my arms behind my head. "Returning the favor of an uninvited visit."

As she hung her purse on a hook adjacent to the front door, her gaze flitted around the room. I'd spent the last hour rifling through her kitchen cabinets, the makeshift desk pushed against the living room wall and her bedroom. For someone in her mid-twenties, she hadn't accumulated much stuff. Needless to say, I didn't find anything of interest in her home. Either she lived a tediously boring life, or she routinely discarded every last piece of personal information. My instincts told me Trinity had something to hide. But didn't we all?

She placed a small brown paper bag on the rectangular, glass entry table and leaned her shoulder against the wall. "I see that. I'm sorry you wasted your time."

"So, tell me." I propped my leather-soled boots onto the metal coffee table resembling a steel drum. A loud thud boomed throughout the room. "Did you tell your boyfriend I already passed along the thumb drives?"

"I did." She licked her lower lip and glanced to the side, a tan colored cat slipping between her legs, then scurrying down the hallway. That cat had been driving me crazy for the past hour, hissing at me and stalking me from room to room. "And stop referring to him as my boyfriend," she added. "He's a business associate. That's it."

I chuckled. "I bet he blew up when you told him the thumb drives were gone."

She pushed away from the wall and took a few steps toward me. The thick cream rug swallowed up the clattering noise of her heels. "Nobody likes to fail. Miles isn't any different."

"True, but I'm sure it's worse when his ass is on the line." I tapped my finger against my lips. "Tell me. Did he pout or throw a tantrum?"

Her eyes narrowed fractionally, and she folded her arms across her torso. "Why do you care?"

Placing my feet back on the floor, I leaned forward, planting my hands on the tops of my knees. "Jones, tell me what you know about the content of those thumb drives."

She shrugged, but I didn't miss the anger flash across her face before she could suppress it. "I don't know anything. It's not my job to know."

I clicked my tongue against the roof of my mouth twice. "And that's where you're going to get yourself into trouble."

Deep lines marred the smooth skin above the bridge of her nose. "What's that supposed to mean?"

I stood and circled the coffee table once before I addressed her question. "You should never agree to a job unless you know every person involved and their motives."

"Miles screens the clients. He makes sure we don't jump into anything…" She paused for a flash of a second as though she couldn't find the right word. "Unsavory."

I barked out a laugh. "Everything about Miles is unsavory."

"You're entitled to your opinion." She flicked her hand dismissively, her red iridescent fingernails catching the light. "But I know for a fact Miles makes sure we stay on the right side of the law."

I pressed my lips together. "There are so many things wrong about that statement, I don't know where to start."

"Go ahead," she said wearily. "I know you're dying to tell me exactly what you think." When I didn't respond, she rolled her eyes. "I don't have all night. Either finish your lecture or let me go to sleep. I'm ready for this day to end."

"Let me make this simple." I blew out a breath, trying to release some of the frustration boxed inside my chest. Miles had thwarted my moves for months now. I was damn sick of it. "Do you trust Miles to make the right decision every single time? Because that's what you're saying when you follow him blindly."

Cringing, she ducked her head as she chewed on her lower lip. She looked so defeated. I closed the space between us and lifted her chin, forcing her to look at me when she answered. Instead, she blinked her eyes what seemed like a hundred times, then closed them as if she were pained.

My gut knotted with concern. What this woman did or didn't do shouldn't matter to me. Life wasn't a picnic. People needed to look out for their interests because, at the end of the day, there were very few people who cared if you sink or swim. For some reason, I cared what happened to Trinity Jones. Twisted as it was, I couldn't stop thinking about her from the moment she strutted into Lang's study with her gun pointed at me. I was self-aware enough to realize I was interested in her on more than a professional level. Too bad—warm, fuzzy feelings chock full of sentiment didn't have a place in my life.

I came here tonight for one reason. I hadn't found enough information on the thumb drives from Lang's computer to force him to resign, but I had a feeling Miles had all the information I needed. If I convinced Trinity to flip sides without alerting Miles, I could wrap up this case. I'd been chasing dead ends from Moscow to D.C. and everywhere in between for over six months. Jack hadn't wanted me to take this mission, and I refused to stop now that I was so close. It slowly evolved from a paycheck into an obsession.

If I had to use the attraction simmering between Trinity and me to succeed, I'd do it. But I had to be smart about it for a couple of reasons. Most importantly, I needed to find out how much she actually knew about this case and whether she had a vested interest in the outcome, other than her job.

Second, Trinity wasn't like any woman I knew. Generally, I lumped the women in my life into two categories—women who wanted a no-strings fuck and women who wanted marriage. I sought out the former and avoided the latter like the plague. Trinity didn't fit neatly into either category and that alone gave me pause about my course of action.

She swallowed, and her throat bobbed up and down. I could tell she was lost somewhere in her memories. "No," she admitted, her chocolate colored eyes popping open. "I don't trust him. Not completely."

I rubbed my hand down the side of my face. "That's good. Miles is on the wrong side of this deal with Lang's computer."

"But I don't trust you either." Her tone was hard and unyielding. "So if you're done searching my home, you can leave."

I threaded my fingers through my hair, frustrated. "Fine, but do me a favor."

Her nose scrunched up in disgust. "What's that?"

"Ask Miles why the information on Lang's computer is so important to him. Ask him how Speaker Benton is involved."

She sucked in a breath, and her spine

straightened. Silence wrapped around us, pressing against my chest like a hundred pound weight. "His client hired him to do a job. I didn't get what he needed. It doesn't look good. There's nothing else to it."

A bitter chuckle spilled from my lips. "This is about more than doing a good job for a client. I know it and I think, deep down, you know it too. What were you instructed to do with the information from Lang's computer?"

She stared out the window over my shoulder. "He wanted me to destroy the thumb drives, then upload a virus onto the computer." Her voice was barely audible, but somehow her words had the impact of a grenade tossed into a crowded room.

"Do you want me to tell you why he asked you to do that?"

She turned her attention back to me, and the force of her gaze speared me. She didn't answer right away. Instead, her eyes hardened. "You mean the truth as you understand it?"

"No, the unqualified truth."

"There's no such thing as an unqualified truth."

I searched her eyes. What happened to this woman to make her so cynical? "Of course there is."

"No, there's perception, interpretation, and wishful thinking. When you bundle all of that together, you get shades of the truth."

Irritated with her and myself, I jammed my hands into my pockets. I glanced around her narrow townhome, taking in all the nearly non-existent details. One picture of Trinity and a younger woman resembling her sat on an otherwise empty fireplace mantle. There wasn't a single decorative pillow on the gray sofa. The only splash of personality came from the yellow accent wall. If not for minimal clothes tucked away in the closet and the personal hygiene products in the bathroom drawers, I'd think no one lived here. I needed to dig a little more into her background to understand her strengths and weaknesses.

I stepped around her and opened the front door. "Well, when you're ready to hear the truth, you know where to find me."

***

"Did you find anything?" Jack said, spinning around in his chair.

I tossed my car keys on the conference table. "Nothing. Her home has fewer personal effects than a hotel room."

Jack snorted. "Miles trained her well."

"I don't know about that. I got the impression her lack of personal effects had more to do with her personal preference than professional necessity."

"Hmm." He tapped his pen on his thigh.

"What about you?" I propped my hip on the corner of the desk. "Did you find out anything else about her?"

"Not much beyond the basic facts." He folded his hands on top of the desk. "Her uncle raised her. She moved to D.C. days after she turned twenty-one. Her younger sister goes to college in Texas a half hour from their hometown. It looks like Trinity pays the tuition. The mom is MIA, and a dad isn't listed on her birth certificate." He shrugged. "No deep, dark, dirty secrets as far as I can tell, but I'll keep digging."

A big part of her story was missing, which made me hesitant to trust her. Trinity acted tough, but it felt like an illusion or a shell to hide all the emotional scars beneath the surface. Sure, she was strong and independent. The fact that Miles took her under his wing and trained her was a testament to her intelligence and potential. Miles was a lot of things, but dumb wasn't one of them. He didn't waste his time on average people. My instincts told me to roll the dice on her, but I didn't know if my attraction to her was overruling my common sense.

"What about the thumb drives? Did you find anything else?"

"Honestly." He ran his fingers through his already disheveled hair. "I just started digging though the information an hour ago."

My eyebrows knitted together as I spotted the half empty bottle of beer next to his computer. "What am I missing? What aren't you telling me?"

He blew out a breath. "Miles was waiting for me when I left the office for lunch."

"Fuck," I hissed.

Jack nodded. "My thoughts exactly."

"What happened?"

"Not much. You know Miles. He never comes right out and says anything. He infers stuff."

I stared out the window over Jack's head. Clouds dotted the otherwise clear skyline. "I know."

"He acted like it was a coincidence." He waved

his arm in one giant swoop. "He said he was just walking around looking for a place to eat lunch. Then the ass had the balls to ask me to join him."

I peered at him, my eyebrow scaling my forehead. "Did you?"

"Hell no. After the shit he's put us through over the last couple of months, I'd strangle him within twenty minutes." He shook his head from side to side. "But I was tempted so I could hear more of his bullshit and try to figure out what he wanted."

"Yeah." I tugged on the sleeves of my shirt. "So what do you think he's up to?"

He scrubbed his hand down the side of his face. "He asked if business was good. He mentioned he heard you took a trip to Moscow last month. Then he babbled about Trinity Jones for a few minutes."

"That son of a bitch. Of course, he knew about Moscow." I went to Moscow to get information about Dima Antonov, the person I suspected of hiring Miles to orchestrate the whole blackmail scheme. Antonov was a Russian businessman involved in a lot of nefarious shit.

Unfortunately, my trip wasn't successful. All of the people I interrogated were careful not to give up anything. I could've used more forceful techniques—ones that violated the United Nations Convention Against Torture and the Geneva Conventions—but I didn't want to risk being detained by Russian authorities if Antonov got wind of my presence. He had enough government authorities in his pocket to make my life uncomfortable.

He nodded. "Yeah, and that means he knows you

didn't get squat while you were there."

"What did he say about Trinity?"

His gaze collided with mine and his lips curled up at the corners. "Nothing special. He casually mentioned they were more than business associates. Then he laughed about your run-in with her at Lang's house. He apologized for attempting to poach our work but said business was business and not to have any hard feelings."

"And what'd you say?"

"I told him we got what we needed, but he should stay the hell away from us, and do his own dirty work."

I nodded. "Good."

"That's where things went south. He said he'd do whatever it took to take us down." He cocked his head to the side. "Well, you in particular. Apparently, I'll be collateral damage if I continue to associate with you."

I balled my hands into fists. "Yeah, well, I feel the same way about him. I won't be happy until I find a way to put him behind bars for the foreseeable future."

He tipped up the bottle of beer, emptying the last half in one swallow. I shook my head. Jack rarely drank like that. "I know," he finally said. "Just be careful. I think he's getting desperate."

"We've talked about this. It means we're getting close."

"Possibly." He wiped a hand over his mouth. "He also told me to tell you to stay the hell away from Trinity."

"That's too bad because I have plans for her."

"Dammit, Knox," he muttered under his breath. "That's what I was afraid of."

My grin widened. "Don't worry about it. Just keep reviewing the documents from Lang's computer and I'll take care of the rest."

He shook his head. "Miles is going to freak. Remember what happened with his ex-wife."

I raised my hands in mock surrender. "That was a mistake. I didn't have a clue who she was, and nothing happened. She's crazy. She sought me out because of Miles's never-ending need to compete with me."

Jack pursed his lips. "I know, but Miles probably doesn't see it that way."

"Miles is a jackass."

He burst out laughing. "I've never heard truer words."

CHAPTER EIGHT

Trinity

For twenty-four hours, I avoided everyone.
Miles.
Faith.
Leslie.
Knox.
I locked myself in my townhome and refused to answer my phone. I didn't have a choice. After Knox left, my mind wouldn't stop spinning in circles, and for the first time in over six months, I knew I needed to talk to Speaker Derrick Benton, my half-brother. We didn't talk much any longer. Recently, he hadn't made much effort to stay in contact. It wasn't unexpected. We didn't grow up together. In fact, I didn't even know he existed until right before I turned twenty-one.

He sent me letter after letter. When I didn't respond, he showed up at my uncle's house. Basically, he'd been nominated for Speaker of the House, and he didn't want me to reveal our connection. I nearly laughed in his face. Before he made contact with me, I didn't even know anything other than my dad's first name, Richard, and I didn't have any interest in seeking out a man who didn't want to be part of my life.

In short, I promised to keep our parentage a secret, and in exchange, Derrick helped me out financially on occasion. At his insistence, I relocated to D.C. He found my townhome and paid the security deposit. He gave me enough money for a down payment on a car three years ago. Simply put, he handed me the rare opportunity to reinvent myself without the demons of my past nipping at my heels. For that alone, I owed him even if he decided he didn't want to be a part of my life anymore.

When I started dating Miles, I occasionally ran into him at political events, but we never acknowledged each other in public. It was better that way. He didn't want to call attention to our dad's infidelities, and I didn't want to call attention to myself.

I had to call three consecutive times before he answered.

"Hello." His voice was stiff and icy.

"It's Trinity," I blurted out, my voice shaky.

"I know. Hold on one second." I heard a puff of air as his hand or something else muffled the speaker of the phone.

I bounced my leg up and down, watching the clock on my nightstand as I waited.

One minute.

The toe of my flat echoed loudly on the

hardwood floors. I should've invested in a rug, but I never bothered. For almost six months, I believed Miles and I would get engaged and I'd move into his house. Once our relationship fell apart, I couldn't bring myself to commit to anything. Emotionally, I was stuck in the mud, not wanting to move forward, but knowing things would never be the same between Miles and me.

Two minutes.

"Asshole," I mumbled under my breath. Derrick had been a complete jerk since I started working for Miles. Our bi-weekly phone calls turned into monthly calls and then stopped almost altogether in the past year.

Three minutes. I pulled the phone away from my ear, intending to disconnect the call when his voice echoed through my bedroom.

"What's going on?" he barked.

"Why aren't you answering your phone?"

"Because I'm in the middle of an important meeting."

"I've called you at least ten times in the last twenty-four hours. I've left you at least three messages. You haven't returned any of my calls," I said, doing little to hide my growing frustration with him.

"What do you need? Money? Help finding a job?"

I squeezed the phone so hard I was surprised it didn't crumble. "No. I have a job, and I sure as hell don't need your money. I mailed you a check two months ago repaying you for everything plus interest. You still haven't cashed it."

"I don't want you to pay me back. The money was a gift. It was the least I could offer, considering…" He fell silent like he couldn't bring himself to utter the words teetering on his lips. He hated talking about the circumstances of my childhood. It was almost as if he couldn't stand to taint his beautiful life with the ugliness of mine.

Sucking in a deep breath through my nose, I bit the inside of my cheek to stifle the urge to blurt out a sarcastic response. "Cash the check, Derrick." Despite what he said, I knew the money wasn't intended as a string-free gift. I considered it hush money even though he'd never admit it. "I'm not going to tell anyone that your dad couldn't keep his pants zipped. I have no interest in being associated with *him*."

Richard Benton, my biological father, made a fortune talking and writing about the importance of being an honorable person. He preached and preached until he was blue in the face, but he didn't think it was necessary for him to heed his own advice. I was proof of it—a walking, talking, breathing stain on his shiny legacy, my half-brother's career, and the illustrious Benton family.

"Then what's going on? I don't have time to chat right now."

Anger fired inside my chest, but I pushed it back. "You haven't called me in months, and you still don't have a few minutes to spare for me?"

Heavy breaths puffed through the phone, and I could imagine the frustration lining his normally serene face. "Just spit it out, Trinity," he hissed. "I'm not in the mood for games. I'm having a bad week."

"Fine." I rubbed the back of my neck. "I ran into someone a couple of days ago, and your name came up in conjunction with Representative Lang. I got the impression something problematic was going on. Is there anything I should know?"

"Are you asking me this or does this question come from your boyfriend?" he snarled.

I dug my free hand into my duvet cover. "We broke up."

"Are you still working for him?"

"Yes, but I didn't hear anything from him."

For a moment, he didn't respond, and I thought he hung up. "Tell me, Trinity. Did you tell Miles that we are related?"

"No," I yelled, irritation mixed with sleep deprivation making my voice sharper and angrier than I had intended. "Absolutely not. I told him I never met my biological father. He didn't ask anything else."

"Are you sure about that?"

Derrick could be such a pompous ass. I didn't know why I bothered with him.

"Yes, Derrick. I have never told anyone about our connection, and I have no intention of sharing that little detail anytime soon." I shook my head. "I don't want anyone's pity."

A weary sigh whistled through the phone. "Okay. I believe you."

I cleared my throat. "Does someone know about me? Is that why you're asking?"

"Yeah."

My heart stuttered. "Oh shit," I whispered.

"What are you going to do?"

"My people are working on it, but I can't promise anything. I might need you to publicly deny our connection at some point."

I nodded even though he couldn't see me. "What does this have to do with Miles? Do you think he knows about us?"

"I'm not sure, but I don't trust him. That's why I've limited our contact over the last year."

"You're the second person to tell me that in the last week," I mumbled, mostly to myself.

"What'd you say?" he asked.

"Nothing," I answered.

"Just be careful what you say to people."

I stood, pacing back and forth along the side of my bed. "And why's that?"

"I'm just trying to warn you to be vigilant," he said, his voice flat.

"Did something happen?" I lowered my voice like someone could overhear me on the street outside of my townhome.

"I can't talk about it on the phone."

"Oh." I chewed on my lower lip. "Do you want to meet in person?"

"I don't think that's a good idea. I don't want anyone to see us together right now."

I rubbed the sudden ache in my chest. I understood why Derrick didn't like to be seen with me, but it hurt. I didn't have much of a family. Despite my best attempts, Faith and I had never been close. I worked hard to give her the things I didn't have growing up, but lately, she seemed more entitled than grateful for all the sacrifices I made for her. My uncle only called me on holidays and birthdays, but I'd do anything for him. When I met Derrick, I thought he'd fill the hole in my heart. For a while it seemed that way, but like everyone else in my life, he had disappointed me.

"Yeah, sure. I get it. Don't worry about it." My voice trembled despite my attempts to pretend it didn't matter.

He exhaled loudly. "I'll stop by your apartment tomorrow night. It won't be until late. After ten. Maybe later."

"What about Ellen? Won't she wonder where you are?" Ellen was his wife of eight years. I'd never met her. I'd seen her in pictures, but our paths had never crossed. Not that it'd matter. As far as I knew, Ellen didn't know about me.

"She's going to her parents' house for dinner tomorrow night. I'll tell her I have to work late."

"Oh. Okay. I'll see you tomorrow." He disconnected the call without responding.

CHAPTER NINE

Knox

"How are things progressing with Trinity?" Jack asked.

He looked a little worse for the wear this week. He had bags under his eyes and more than his customary day or two's worth of whisker growth on his face. His clothes were wrinkled, and I could swear he'd been wearing the same jeans for the past week.

I scooped up my keys and jammed them in my front pocket. "They're not."

He snickered. "Why not?"

"She hasn't gone anywhere in days."

Sharp creases dented the skin between his brows. "Why not?"

"I don't know." I crossed the room. "I won't be in the office tomorrow. I have a security update I need to do for Black Investments."

"No problem." He closed his laptop and stuffed it into his tan messenger bag. The thing was ancient.

Threads dangled from the seams, and the bottom looked more black than tan. He'd been carrying it since his days in the Navy. "You want to grab a drink at the bar down the street?"

"I can't." I opened the door, and Jack followed me out.

"Do you have a date?"

"Nope." I pressed the call button for the elevator. "I'm going to swing by Trinity's place."

"What for?"

"I don't know. I guess I'm going to do a little surveillance." I winked as we stepped into the elevator. "See what she's been up to."

He rolled his eyes. "We have people to do that shit. You don't have to do it yourself."

"I know, but it's not that far out of my way."

He smirked. "Uh-huh."

I shoved his shoulder. "Back off. We need her help."

"There are alternatives."

I stepped off the elevator and pressed the unlock button on my key fob. "Yep, and I'll pursue those if this doesn't work."

***

I sat in my car outside of Trinity's home. She lived on the main floor of a gray three-story brownstone near the National Mall. An hour into my surveillance, a man in a long, black overcoat jogged down the street with his head angled toward the sidewalk. A dark fedora shaded his face from view.

He took an abrupt right and ran up the steps to Trinity's home. Without hesitating, he knocked on her door. Seconds later, she opened the door and waved him inside. He handed her his hat and glanced over his shoulder.

"I'll be damned," I muttered, leaning forward to get a better view. "What the hell is he doing here?"

After the door had closed, I filled the inside of my car with a string of colorful curses. What was wrong with me? My gut ached like someone had dropkicked me in the stomach, and I knew exactly what I was feeling—jealousy. I could ignore it. I could dismiss it. I could pretend it didn't bother me, but I knew the truth. From the first moment I saw her, Trinity had become an obsession. Regardless of what I did, I couldn't get her out of my head. Either I was intensely attracted to her and needed to fuck her out of my brain or she brought out something in me I hadn't felt with any other woman. I didn't like either scenario. Being dependent on anyone for any reason didn't sit well with me.

Ten minutes ticked by like an hour, and I broke down and I called Jack. I needed to talk to him because I felt like I was coming out of my skin.

"Hello," he said, answering his phone after the first ring. I heard the rumble of voices and pounding music in the background.

"Can you talk?" I asked.

"One second. Let me step outside." When the music and voices faded, he continued. "What's going on?"

I squeezed the steering wheel with one hand until my knuckles whitened. "I'm not sure, but Benton just showed up at Trinity Jones's house."

"What the fuck? What's going on?"

I shook my head. "I don't have a clue. Either Miles is using Trinity to communicate with Benton or Trinity is working with Benton."

"Or she's having an affair with Benton."

"I don't know. Benton and his wife seem pretty solid. Other than the blackmail scandal brewing around him for the past year, he's kept his nose clean."

"This is ridiculous, Knox. Do you hear yourself? We both know Benton is up to his eyeballs in shit. He refused to bring up another bill for vote in the House just this week. Getting involved with this woman who may or may not be backstabbing Miles or fucking Benton on the side is a bad idea for so many reasons. There are other ways to unravel this mess. We don't need her."

"Yeah, maybe you're right." I rubbed my temples, my gaze glued to Trinity's home. I didn't know what I thought I'd see.

"Not maybe. I am right. This girl is trouble. First, she's connected to Miles, and that's reason enough to stay away from her, but now she's fucking Benton and—"

"We don't know that," I snapped, interrupting him. "They could be friends or she could be working with him."

He exhaled. "A man only drops by a single woman's house at ten-thirty at night for one reason and it's not to paint each other's fingernails or share stories about their day at work."

I glanced at the yellow light glowing like a

beacon from a large picture window at the front of her townhome. The possibility of catching a glimpse of her tonight made me decline Jack's invitation to go out for a drink. What had this woman done with my balls?

"I'm not stupid. I realize that," I muttered as the shiny red door of her townhome opened. Shadows shrank as the interior light spilled onto her front steps.

Benton stepped over the threshold. Her head moved up and down, and he leaned in, whispering something in her ear. Almost immediately, he engulfed her in a one-armed hug, which didn't offer any insight into the nature of their relationship.

"He's leaving," I said.

"Are you going to follow him?"

"No."

"There's still time to meet me for a drink."

I tapped my fingers on my thigh, staring at Trinity's townhouse. "Where are you? I could use a drink."

"I'm at Mercy."

Trinity closed the curtains of her front window, and her home faded to black. "No," I said, changing my mind instantly. "I have a shit load of work tomorrow, and I need a clear head."

"Are you going to look into the connection between Trinity and Benton?"

"I will."

"Good. Call me tomorrow if you need anything."

"Will do." I disconnected the call.

I sat in the car for nearly an hour before something compelled me to go inside. I needed answers, and somehow I convinced myself seeing her would tell me what I wanted to know.

Not long after, I stood at the foot of her bed watching her sleep. She had left her closet door cracked open and a bar of light lit the lower half of her face. One of her legs had slipped out from beneath the white sheets. She wore a faded black t-shirt that barely covered her panties. Her mink colored hair fanned her pillow. Her face was scrubbed clean of makeup, and a small smattering of freckles dusted her nose.

For a fleeting second, I pictured sliding into bed next her and stripping off her clothes.

I imagined what she looked like naked.

I wondered how her hair smelled.

I speculated how she'd taste as I explored every inch of her long, toned body.

Then I shut down the fantasy as fast as possible. I was treading a slippery slope. I needed to snap out of it and stay focused on the end goal.

Slipping out of her room, I quietly searched the house, investigating all areas I failed to check the previous time and double-checking others. Empty-handed, I snuck out the front door nearly an hour later.

CHAPTER TEN

Trinity

Sweat snaked down my spine. My thighs burned, and my chest heaved as the soles of my gray and orange sneakers slapped against the red brick sidewalk at six-thirty in the morning. Growing up, I always dodged the cracks. It was a habit I picked up as a kid after my mom disappeared. As ridiculous as it sounded, taking the silly children's game to heart and avoiding the cracks was the only thing I could do to keep my mom safe. I'd never been able to shake the compulsion. The brick sidewalks of Capitol Hill made it impossible to play the game.

Faint pink and red brushstrokes still painted the horizon, softening the hard edges of all the buildings. It was my favorite time of the day. Some people loved twilight. Some people loved the night. I loved the morning, especially those few hours where the city was still sleepy and the day was filled with infinite possibilities.

I mouthed the words to "Fight Song" by Rachel

Platten as they blasted from my earbuds for at least the sixth time since I started running. It seemed more than a little trite, but I needed all the courage I could get to show up on Miles's doorstep this morning. Even though Derrick begged me to stay away from Miles and distance myself from his problems, I refused. I needed to help Derrick. He helped me start a new life in D.C., and I wanted to help him now. Besides, I didn't want the media to drag me through the mud because someone revealed my connection to the Bentons.

It took me twenty minutes to jog to Miles's house from mine. With my hands braced on the tops of my thighs and the wire from my earbuds draped over my shoulder, I stood in front of his lacquered black front door. When my breathing returned to normal, I rapped on the door. I could've used my key, but it would give him the impression that we'd get back together at some point. While creating that illusion might've been useful to help Derrick, I couldn't bring myself to let it happen. After what Derrick told me, the thought of inviting his touch or kissing him made my stomach roll.

Miles's daughter flung open the door. She propped one of her hands on her hip and flipped her long blonde hair behind her shoulder. Even though I had at least six inches on her, she managed to look down her nose at me.

"What do you want?"

"Hi." I smiled brightly as I slid my chunky sunglasses onto the top of my head. "I need to talk to your dad. Is he around?"

"Yeah, but he's not up yet. I'll tell him you were

here."

As she moved to close the door, I shoved my foot into the opening and smacked the palm of my hand against the door. "It's important. This can't wait. Can you get him?" I peered over her shoulder, trying to catch a glimpse of Miles.

Just then, her phone buzzed. "Hold on," she mumbled, pulling it out of her pocket and walking into the living room.

Using her momentary distraction to my advantage, I sailed inside and darted down the hall. Taking a deep breath, I pushed open the door to his bedroom.

"Wait, he's not alone," his daughter yelled from the living room, but it was too late.

Shock vibrated through my chest, and I clutched the doorjamb to stop myself from collapsing. Time freeze-framed as I surveyed the scene in front of me. Miles's bare ass was in the air, pumping furiously back and forth. His ex-wife was on all fours, her too long yellowish-blonde hair extensions swaying back and forth.

Air expelled from my lungs with a whistle like a deflating balloon. His hips froze mid-pump. In slow motion, he turned his head, his gaze colliding with mine.

"Oh my God," I muttered, at a loss for words.

Sasha, his ex-wife, snickered.

"Shit!" Miles yelled, without making any effort to untangle himself. "What are you doing here?"

My morning coffee threatened to make an appearance on the floor, so I turned my back to the scene. "I texted you last night, remember?" When he didn't answer, I continued talking. "I needed to talk to you about work, and go over some details, but I don't think that'll be necessary now. I'm done here."

Poison dripped from my words. I couldn't believe I considered letting Miles back into my life, no matter how transitory the thought. Even though I didn't want him, it hurt to catch him in yet another lie. My mind whirled with the sheer number of fabrications and half-truths he'd probably told me over the last few years. This moment tainted everything about our relationship.

"Wait." I heard the sheets rustle and his bare feet thump against the floor. "Let me explain."

"It's not necessary. Go ahead and finish." Pressure built behind my eyes, begging to trickle down my face. Inhaling and exhaling slowly, I willed it away, refusing to give him the satisfaction. When I regained control of my body, I slammed the door and fled down the hallway. My heart thudded like a drum in my ears, louder and louder as my sneaker-clad feet devoured the distance between the front door and me.

But I didn't move fast enough. A foot from the door, his fingers hooked into my shoulders and he spun me around. Luckily, he had managed to slip on a pair of plaid pajama pants before he chased me. "Tri," he said, his voice hushed.

"Don't call me that," I snapped. When he started calling me Tri a few months after we met, I'd loved it. Nobody cared enough about me to give me a nickname before I met Miles. It made me feel special, cared for, and loved. Now, the thought of the time I had wasted on his deceitful ass made me want to rip the hair out of his head, strand by strand.

He pursed his lips as he adjusted the waistband of his pants. "Fine, but at least give me the opportunity to explain."

"Miles," I said, drawing out his name. "I'm not a five-year-old. What I just saw doesn't need an explanation."

He opened and then immediately closed his mouth because he knew I was right. I'd caught him mid-act. He couldn't deny it happened.

"That's what I thought." I wiggled out of his hold and took a few steps backward. "Have a nice life, Miles."

His brows pinched together. "What's that supposed to mean?"

I drew in a shuddering breath. "You can consider this my resignation." A pain stabbed through my chest when the words exited my mouth, but I didn't have a choice. I needed to jump off this emotional rollercoaster while I still could. I'd already invested too much time in him.

"You can't walk away from this job. You need the money."

I shrugged and painted a tight smile on my face. "Leslie will give me a job at the bar until I find something else. I'll survive. I always do."

"How are you going to pay your bills and Faith's tuition? You need me. You need this job."

Rage set my nerve endings on fire, and my hand whipped through the air of its own volition. My open palm crashed against the side of his face. A loud crack reverberated through the room. I couldn't believe he'd used my fears against me.

He cupped the side of his face, his eyes glittering with rage. "What the hell was that, Trinity?"

"That," I pointed my finger at him, "is for being a liar, a user, and an all-around piece of shit."

He took a step forward, frustration creasing his forehead and a vein near his temple pulsing.

"Stay the hell away from me," I said through clenched teeth. "I'm done with you. I'm done with this job. I never want to see you again."

"You're not done until I say you're done. You owe me."

"I don't owe you a damn thing," I snarled, as I curled my hand around the doorknob behind me.

His lips quirked up at the corners. "You'd be nowhere without me."

My gaze flicked to the side. Miles's daughter and his ex-wife—current lover or whatever the hell she was—stood in the living room, staring at the scene unfolding in front of them. His daughter looked horrified. Sasha had a smug, self-satisfied smile stretching her overly plump lips across her face. She was gloating. Instead of anger, I felt pity.

Pity for her.

Pity that she hadn't walked away from Miles years ago.

Pity that she actually thought this fight gave her an opening to have Miles all to herself.

I suspected Sasha was an enabler, not a victim, of her ex-husband's affairs. They played a game of tug of war with their affections. She pushed him away. He found someone new, and she fought to win him back. Then it started all over again. He'd replace me soon enough. In fact, I didn't know why he kept me around as long as he did. It didn't make sense. When we were together, we were better friends than lovers. We lacked passion. If our relationship had a pulse line, it would've been nearly flat with a few miniature upward ticks.

Flinging open the door, I shook my head. "After everything you put me through, I think I can safely call us even."

His chest heaved and he pinned me with his narrowed gaze. "If you walk out the door right now, don't expect me to pay you for the last job."

A shot of disbelieving laughter exploded from my lips. My hand twitched with the urge to hit him again, but I dug deep inside myself and located my last ounce of self-control. "Keep the fucking money. I don't want it." I stepped outside, shutting the door behind me.

Suppressed tears beaded on my lashes, spilling down my face as my vision swam. The feelings of unworthiness, rejection, and despair I'd been holding back hit me with the force of a roundhouse kick. I clutched the railing to keep from falling to my knees. Good or bad, over the years I'd gotten used to Miles's constant presence in my life. He'd become my boss, my friend, my confidant, and eventually my lover.

Why did he lie to me over and over?

I shook my head to clear my mind. None of this mattered. We were over before we ever started, and I never really loved him. I didn't think I'd ever understand his motivations for pulling me into his life when he never intended to end his relationship with his ex-wife.

At least I hadn't succumbed to his manipulative attempts to get back together. That would've made today even more humiliating. Right now, I needed to focus on rebuilding my life, and staying true to myself in the process.

CHAPTER ELEVEN

Knox

As I rounded the corner of my street, Trinity pushed away from the wall of my building. She wore a long black coat and black boots. The glow from the overhead lamppost highlighted the soft fall of her hair over her shoulders. Her dark gaze collided with mine, and I paused, reluctant to deal with her right now. She already monopolized too many of my thoughts today, and I hadn't gotten anything done.

Archer would light a fire under my ass when he found out I didn't bother installing the security updates for Black Investments, but I couldn't concentrate on his company right now. I'd spent more than half of the day digging into her background, trying to ferret out her secrets. I wanted to know every little thing about Trinity Jones.

Did she prefer coffee or tea?

How many men had she dated?

Who were her parents?

Did she have any siblings?

What were her hobbies?

How much money did she have in her bank accounts?

How much credit card debt did she have?

I called in favors from acquaintances. I hacked into secure databases. I went through her cell phone records. And after nearly five hours of searching, I hadn't found much of anything, except that her relationship with Benton predated her association with Miles. Lamentably, even with all the information I sourced, I couldn't determine the exact nature of their relationship.

On at least two separate occasions, Benton had wired money into her bank accounts. Combined, the money transfers exceeded fifteen thousand dollars. As far as I could ascertain, she had never repaid the money. Granted, fifteen thousand dollars was nothing for Benton. He probably spent that much on a week's worth of his custom suits, but it was a lot for a woman like Trinity Jones. All evidence pointed to an extra-marital affair, rather than a friendship, but her phone records indicated they didn't communicate frequently.

I balled my hands into fists as my legs erased the distance between us.

"Trinity," I said, her name tumbling off my tongue with detached coolness. As if she hadn't starred in my dreams for the past two nights. As if I never imagined tangling my hands in her long dark hair as I moved inside of her. "Why are you here?"

She angled her head in the direction of the door

to my building. "Can we move this conversation inside?"

"No," I said, clenching my jaw. "If you want to talk to me, then start talking because I'm not inviting you into my home." I didn't want her in my home unless and until I thought I could trust her to some degree.

She tipped her head to the sky for a beat, apparently considering whether to continue the conversation or walk away. "Fine. Have it your way." She cocked her hip to the side. "I'm ready to hear the truth about Lang and Benton."

I scrubbed my hand down the side of my face. She wanted the truth, but I couldn't tell her much of anything before I understood her connection to Benton. "Why should I tell you the truth now? You had your chance."

She shifted on her feet, but I couldn't tell what she was thinking. "I don't work for Miles anymore. Does that change your mind?"

I laced my hands behind my head, struggling to decide how to handle this development. "Since when?" I asked, my voice gruff.

"Since this morning," she said, her face inscrutable, her eyes like onyx.

I stuffed my hands into my pockets, staring at the clogged traffic in front of my building. The blare of horns filled my ears. People veered around us, caught up in their own lives. I rolled back my shoulders. "I'll need verification."

"Here." She dipped her hand into her coat pocket and clutched her phone in the palm of her hand. "You can read our texts from today."

My brows pinched together. "You quit by text?"

"No." She entered her password and waved the phone. "I quit in person, but he's been texting me all day. Take a look for yourself."

I snatched the phone out of her hand.

Miles: Come back here. We weren't done talking.

Trinity: I'm not interested in anything you have to say.

Miles: You didn't give me any notice. I won't give you a recommendation if you walk away like this.

Trinity: Perfect. I'm not asking for one. I don't want anything from you. We're done.

Miles: I don't accept your resignation.

Trinity: I'm blocking your number. Don't contact me again.

The messages went back and forth at least five more times before they stopped entirely.

"Okay, I get the point." I shoved the phone back into her hand. "What happened?"

She exhaled loudly. "It's stupid. I don't want to talk about it."

"Then I can't tell you anything."

"Fine." She rolled her eyes. "I walked in on him screwing his ex-wife this morning."

I arched my eyebrows. "I thought you weren't dating him."

"I wasn't. He wanted to get back together." She folded her arms across her chest. "But he told me things were over between them, yet again. He's been pressuring me to give him a second chance since we broke up, but he won't push her out of his life."

"Yeah, I'd stay clear from them." I shook my head. "They're one fucked up couple. I'm not very fond of Miles, and Sasha is absolutely crazy."

Twin lines bracketed the side of her mouth as she pursed her lips. "Do you know Sasha?"

I mock shivered. "Let's just say, I've had the distinct displeasure of running into her a few times, and I go the other direction any time I see her."

Her lips tugged downward and her cute nose crinkled. "Should I ask for an explanation?"

"No. Definitely not," I said, dryly as I gestured to the glass door of my building. "Let's go inside."

She forced a weak smile, the small action warming her brown eyes fractionally, and damn if I didn't feel a spark of uninvited attraction. "I thought you'd never ask. I've been standing out here for an hour, and my feet are completely numb."

"Well, Jones." I chuckled. "We wouldn't want that."

I believed she broke up with Miles, but I didn't know how long it'd last. Everything Jack told me about their relationship indicated Miles wouldn't let her go easily. I could handle Miles, but I still didn't know what to make of her relationship with Benton. I needed to see them in the same room together.

Fortunately, I had the perfect way to make it happen and simultaneously put Miles on notice that Trinity wouldn't be working for him any longer.

CHAPTER TWELVE

Trinity

Knox pushed open the door to his apartment. "It's quicker with keys," he said, arching one eyebrow.

"I brought my tools just in case," I said, patting my pocket. "I planned to give you fifteen more minutes before I let myself in."

One corner of his mouth twisted upward. "I guess I need to upgrade the security in my apartment."

"You could do that, but it wouldn't stop me. I've been trained by the best." I followed him inside, pausing near the kitchen. I didn't turn on the lights the last time I came here, so I took a few moments to survey my surroundings. The kitchen and living room were one big space separated by a kitchen counter with three bars stools and a round bistro table. Two beige colored sofas flanked a sliding glass door.

"Miles?" he said, disbelievingly.

"No, my uncle. He believed every woman should know how to pick a lock, shoot a gun, and land a punch."

"Ah. Consider me warned." He dropped his keys on the kitchen counter. "Do you want something to drink?"

My gaze swung to his and I pushed my fingers through my hair. "No. I'm good."

The last thing I needed was to lower my guard around him. I needed his help, but I'd be stupid to trust him. I hadn't figured out his motives yet. Maybe he wanted to help his client…whoever that was. Maybe he hated Miles and wanted to use me to needle him. Maybe he was knee-deep in this mess with Benton. I couldn't be sure. I had to keep my eyes open and my mind clear.

"Are you sure?" He pulled a bottle of white wine from the wine refrigerator beneath the counter and poured himself a liberal portion. He lifted the glass by its stem and swirled it before taking sip. "I'm not going to take advantage of you if that's what you're worried about."

For some strange reason, this man had the ability to read between the lines and piece together everything I was thinking. *Oh God, I hope not everything.* I didn't want him to know the mixed, idiotic tangle of emotions he brought out in me.

"I'm not worried. I can handle myself," I answered, contradicting him.

"Good. Because I don't like to drink alone." He handed me a glass, and damn my wandering eyes for noticing the way his sinewy muscles rippled beneath his fitted navy shirt. "You can sit down," he said, as he sat in a barstool at the kitchen counter.

Nodding, I settled into a chair at the small table instead of sitting next to him. "So, where do you want to start?"

He grinned at me, then took a sip of wine before his gaze swept down my body. It almost felt like a physical touch. "What do you know about Representative Lang?"

I tapped my finger on the table. "Not much. He's a member of the House of Representatives. He's from a district in Northern California. He's married with two kids."

"Right. Now tell me what Miles wanted from his computer."

I bounced my foot up and down, the heels of my shoes clicking against the floor like a typewriter. "Honestly, I don't know. I told you everything I know about it already. Miles keeps me in the dark sometimes."

"I don't believe you," he said archly.

I sucked in a breath. "Look. I know it sounds far-fetched, but according to Miles, I was still in training. Most of the time, we discussed the details, but he was particularly tight-lipped about this deal with Lang. He told me you might show up at the party and that you planned to lift information off Lang's computer. He wanted me to take the thumb drives from you and destroy the computer with a virus."

"That's it?" he prodded, his sapphire eyes cataloging every twitch, blink, and movement I made. "Can you remember anything else?"

I angled my head as I replayed the conversation

with him in my head. "Wait," I said, wringing my hands underneath the table. "He made a passing comment about the stupidity of keeping that kind of evidence on his computer. How it would screw up everything."

He nodded absently, then stood. "I'll be back in a second."

"Sure," I said, watching him walk down the hallway without further explanation.

A few minutes later, he reappeared with a file folder in his hand. "Take a look at this." He dropped it on the table and hunkered down on the chair across from me.

Casually, I guided the file closer to me and flipped open the cover. I flicked through picture after picture of Miles meeting with Representative Lang. One in an alley. One at the National Mall. One on the sidewalk outside of Lang's home.

"So what? They know each other," I said, closing the folder when I reached the last picture. "Miles isn't working for Lang. Otherwise, Lang would've let Miles destroy his computer. He wouldn't have asked me to do it."

"You're right. I think Miles blackmailed Lang into helping him."

My mouth hinged opened. "Blackmailed him with what?"

"That's what I wanted to figure out."

My shoulders slumped. "Did you find anything on the thumb drives?"

He glanced to the side. "Not yet, but I haven't made it through everything."

Feeling unsettled, I swirled the gold bangles on

my wrist. This story sounded eerily similar to what Derrick told me. "Does Miles demand money in exchange for his silence?"

He cupped his chin between his thumb and index finger. His eyes never veered from mine, and I felt the physical weight of his stare all the way down to the tips of my toes. "No. Miles is extorting votes out of members of the House of Representatives."

I crossed and uncrossed my legs, the direction of this conversation making me increasingly uncomfortable. "Why? What would he get out of forcing them to change their votes?"

"I don't think he's doing it for himself. He's working for someone who has a vested interest in certain legislation being passed. I have my suspicions, but I haven't put the pieces together."

I rubbed my suddenly numb fingertips along my thighs. "Why are you telling me this? It seems risky. How do you know I'm not part of this scheme? I could run back to Miles and tell him everything."

"You're right." One side of his lips tugged upward. "I don't know what you're going to do, but I don't care if you tell Miles."

My eyebrows crinkled together. "Why not?"

Bending forward, he braced his elbows on top of the table, his hands a few inches from mine. "I haven't told you anything Miles doesn't know. That's why he sent you to Lang's party to stop me. He knows I'm getting close."

I took a sip of the wine, and I could feel every millimeter of its descent until it hit my stomach like a leaden weight. "What do you want from me?"

"I want you to help me get evidence against

Miles."

"What kind of evidence?"

"I need to know if he is working with anyone else, if he has contacts I don't know about. I want copies of his emails, his bank statements. Everything."

"Why don't you hack into his computer and his phone? Isn't that your specialty?"

His face darkened. "I've been trying, but so far I've been unable to do it. My partner, Jack, is still working on it, but I've been investigating him for six months, and I'm running out of time."

I laced my hands together in my lap. The fact that Miles had such advanced security likely meant he was into some bad stuff, but maybe I was just paranoid and it was a necessary part of his job. "I don't think I can help."

"You know him. You know how he works, and for the most part, he trusts you. You can infiltrate every part of his company and personal life without too much effort."

I snorted. "I don't think so. You saw our text messages. We're over. He wouldn't believe it if I called him and apologized. He's not stupid."

He angled his head to the side. "I know that, but I'm going to make him fight for you. Once he believes he's won you back, you'll have access to everything."

I arched my eyebrows in disbelief. "Right. How are you going to do that?"

A smile spread across his face, and my heart fluttered inside my chest. He was too beautiful; too appealing. "You're going to attend a fundraiser tomorrow night as my date."

I chewed on my lower lip. "And Miles will be there?"

"Yes."

I lowered my gaze. "Why should I help you?"

"Because you need a new job and I'll pay you. If you do a good job, I might have a permanent position for you at the end of this."

"How much?"

He waved his hand dismissively. "Whatever Miles pays you."

Logically, I should run fast and hard from his offer. Nothing good would come of further entangling myself in this situation, but I needed the money. For Faith. For myself. And with any luck, I could help Derrick and figure how to permanently bury any evidence linking me to my biological father.

"Fine. I'll do it." I took another sip of my wine, not feeling the same rush I normally did when assigned a new job. "What's the fundraiser for?"

"It's to raise money for Speaker Benton's reelection."

The wine I'd drunk sloshed uncomfortably in my gut. "Speaker Benton?"

"Yeah." He smiled blandly, but his eyes were alert and probing. "You know him, right?"

My heart came to a grinding halt, and when it resumed, it thumped at a rate of a hundred miles per hour. "No. Not really. I've heard of him, and I've seen him at a few events, but we've never been introduced."

His jaw tightened. "Really? I find that hard to

believe." His tone was cold, and a shiver of unease rippled down my spine. Did he know Derrick and I were related?

"It's the truth," I said, jerking my head up and down like a bobble head doll with an overly bright smile. Folding my hands in my lap, I smoothed my expression, and I mentally slapped myself for being so transparent.

"Huh, that's interesting." He pushed his chair away from the table, and it scraped against the floor. "We'll have to rectify that tomorrow night. By most accounts, he's a relatively likable guy. So is his wife." His eyes narrowed fractionally, and I felt like I had *liar* carved into my forehead.

"What does Benton have to do with Miles and Lang?"

"I'm not entirely sure."

"Oh," I mumbled, my heart squeezing. Eager to get away from him, I scrambled out of my seat. I whipped my phone out of my pocket and opened my calendar. "What's the address of the fundraiser?"

"Don't worry about it. I'll drop by your place at six to pick you up."

I took a step backward, avoiding his gaze. "That's unnecessary. I'll meet you there."

"I insist." Standing, he crossed the room, pausing next to the front door. "Besides, it'll look more convincing if we arrive together. We can't have people suspecting our involvement is a farce."

"Fine," I conceded, sucking in a strangled breath. There was more to his request than that, but questioning him would be futile. He had a practiced blank look on his face that said he had no intention of enlightening me. Besides, if Miles saw me arrive alone, I'd have to face him without Knox's support, and I didn't want to do that. Not yet anyway. I had to unravel all the pieces to protect Derrick and myself. Only then could I turn the tables on Miles.

"By the way." Knox opened his front door. "Has Miles ever mentioned Dima Antonov?"

I frowned. "No. Why?"

He lifted, then dropped his shoulder. "No reason."

"Okay. See you tomorrow."

As I left his apartment, his eyes burned a hole in my back until the elevator opened, and I disappeared inside. Once I was out of his line of sight, the knot in my chest loosened a fraction.

CHAPTER THIRTEEN

Knox

At five minutes after six, I pulled up in front of Trinity's place. The day had been hell. I'd combed through the files I lifted from Lang's computer, and I didn't find a single link between Miles and Lang or Miles and Benton. Then, fifteen minutes before I needed to leave, I stumbled upon a series of encrypted files. Instead diving headfirst into the new obstacle, I packed up and headed home. I knew if I tried to open the files, I wouldn't let myself leave the office for hours, and I had to keep working every angle of this case, which meant moving things forward with Trinity.

With her phone pressed against her ear, she stood on the front steps of her townhome in a curve-hugging black lace dress with a plunging neckline. She wore her hair in a loose braid that hung over her bare shoulder. Her lips were pale, and her eyes were smoky. I couldn't tear my gaze away from her. She looked beautiful.

I jumped out of the car, jogged around the front end, and flung open the passenger side door. "Hi."

She lifted her head, and a big smile spread across her face. My breath stuttered in my chest. Her smile was a weapon of mass destruction.

"You're late," she announced as she dumped her cell phone into her purse and slipped into the passenger seat.

"Sorry. I got caught up at work," I answered once I joined her in the car.

Glancing over my shoulder, I pulled into traffic. Speaker Benton lived in a historic home in northwest D.C, near the Washington National Cathedral. His home had to be worth over ten million dollars. Members of the House of Representatives didn't earn enough money to live like Benton, but he had family money, lots of it. His father, Richard Benton, made millions of dollars writing inspirational books on living with honor and morals. His earnings only added to the already bloated fortune of one of America's wealthiest families. Their holdings included cable, television, radio, and newspapers. They flew under the radar, but they had their fingers in everything. As an only child and the heir to the Benton family fortune, he didn't need to lift a finger for the rest of his life. Instead, he pursued a career as a lifetime politician.

"What's the plan for tonight?" Trinity fidgeted nervously with the gold buckle on the front of her small rectangular purse.

"Nothing special. Just stay glued to my side. I'll introduce you to Derrick Benton and his wife. We'll make small talk. Then we'll leave. We'll be in and out in under an hour."

"Does your plan include confronting Miles?"

"No." I shook my head. "But if he approaches us, we'll have to improvise."

From the corner of my eye, I noticed her entire body tense. "What do you mean by improvise?"

My lips tipped upward. "Well, Jones, I plan to do everything within my power to make a convincing argument that you're with me now. That means touching, kissing." I cocked my head to the side. "You know, the things normal couples do."

I wasn't against a small display of affection to shove our fake relationship in Miles's face. In fact, I looked forward to seizing any opportunity to touch, kiss and do a whole lot more with her.

Her mouth popped open, and her breath rushed out of her mouth. "Are you serious?" she hissed, sounding more appalled than I liked.

"Deadly serious," I answered, my voice cold and flat.

"No." Her hands shaking, she tugged on the hem of her dress. "I will not put on some cheap display in front of a bunch of people I don't know to piss off Miles. I will stand by you. I will follow you around with a big fat smile on my face and pretend I like you. We can even touch each other in the normal course of things, but that's it. I won't do anything else."

"We've kissed before." I grinned, not taking my eyes off the road. "You didn't have a problem with it. Actually, I got the distinct impression you enjoyed it."

She smirked. "You wish."

I chuckled. "Don't lie, Jones. You were so into it. You didn't utter a single word of protest when I took your gun and the thumb drive."

"Like you pointed out at the time, I didn't have any other options. So when you kissed me, I closed my eyes and went along for the ride."

I tightened my hands on the steering wheel. "If it makes you feel better, you can keep telling yourself that, but we both know the truth."

Her grin dimmed. "You know, you're not much of a gentleman. You're kind of an asshole," she said, her voice strangled.

As I turned into the Benton family estate, a steady string of curses rolled through my mind. What a disaster. I needed her compliant, which meant I should be charming her instead of taunting her. She was in a good mood when I picked her up, and now I needed to start all over.

I turned off the car and waved away the valet. "I know. I'm sorry." I shoved my hand through my hair.

"Great," she mocked, her gaze trained out the passenger side window. "Let's get this over with, so I can go home and go to bed." She reached for the door handle, but I grabbed her hand, halting her exit.

"Jones, look at me."

"What do you want?" Her head snapped toward mine and her dark braid whipped around her shoulder. Tears glimmered in her eyes.

Guilt lanced through my chest. "Dammit," I muttered, brushing my knuckles along the side of her face, and she jerked away.

"Don't touch me," she hissed.

"Do you want to know why I kissed you that night?"

She shrugged. "Apparently, because it was expedient."

"Yes, there was that. But mostly because I wanted to kiss you from the first moment you walked through Lang's study door, so forgive me if I'd like to believe we both enjoyed it." I brushed a kiss along the inside of her wrist and released her hand. "Now, are you ready to go inside?"

Her eyes sought out mine and she sighed. "No, but I will."

CHAPTER FOURTEEN

Trinity

I twirled my glass in my hand, smiled politely and responded to questions, but I couldn't take it any longer. Between the speculative glances Derrick's wife aimed in my direction, and the daggers Miles shot me from across the room, I needed a break.

I tugged on the sleeve of Knox's jacket. "I need to go to the bathroom. I'll be right back."

He eyed me suspiciously for a second, then nodded.

I was halfway down the hall when someone grabbed my wrist and whirled me around.

"What are you doing here?" Derrick hissed next to my ear. "I thought we agreed to stay away from each other until this thing cools down."

"Not here," I said, yanking my wrist out of his grasp.

I pushed open a nearby door, pulled him inside and locked it behind us. I glanced around the room.

A large mahogany desk took center stage in the middle of the floor. Sunflower yellow curtains framed the window. A cornflower blue and ivory rug blanketed the floor. We were in his office.

He paced the length of the room, pausing near the window with his hands on his hips. "Why are you here?"

"I didn't have a choice. I left you a message this afternoon warning you. Didn't you get it?"

"No." He rubbed his hands over his face. "Jesus, Trinity, my mother was here."

"I didn't realize," I said, my voice trailing off. "I didn't think—"

His hand slashed through the air. "No, you didn't. My wife is coming out of her skin. She doesn't want you here. She has this crazy idea that someone will notice a family resemblance between us."

I rolled my eyes. "Other than the color of our hair and eyes, we look nothing alike."

His gaze swept over my body. "I don't think so either, but Ellen doesn't agree."

"Great." I folded my arms across my chest. "Well, tell her I'm sorry, and I'll avoid darkening her door from now on. I didn't even think she knew about me."

He glanced at the floor. "She didn't know anything about it until I got that letter," he said, his voice lowering an octave. "The one that started this whole mess."

"Why'd you tell her?"

He raked his hands through his hair. "Because I didn't want her to find out about it through the media if things got ugly."

I leaned against the side of his desk, feeling lightheaded. "We're going to figure a way out of this mess, Derrick."

"Yeah, I don't know. I can't do this much longer. I won't drag my family through the mud. If it doesn't stop soon, I'm going to withdraw from the race. Then they won't be able to hold anything over my head."

"Give me a couple of weeks before you decide. I have a lead. That's why I'm here."

He jammed his hands into his pockets. "What is it?"

"I don't want to talk about it tonight, but I think you're right about Miles." I didn't want anyone to find us in Derrick's study. It'd raise red flags, and people might dig into our connection. If Miles knew Derrick was my half-brother, other people might be able make the connection.

He angled his head to the side. "What do you know?"

"Not much." I pushed away from the desk and moved to the door. "But I think he has something to do with the blackmail scheme. I don't think you're the only victim either."

"Fuck." He pinched the bridge of his nose. "Who else?"

"I don't have any concrete information, but I think Representative Lang is involved, either as a co-conspirator or a victim."

His shoulders tensed, then he gave a jerky nod. "Okay. I'll call you Monday and we'll get together again. I want to know everything."

I tugged on the lapel of his jacket. "Don't spend

the weekend worrying about this. We'll figure something out."

"I won't." He smiled, but it didn't reach his eyes. "How does Knox Black fit into this whole thing?"

Several answers flickered through my mind, but I decided to keep the details to myself. "He doesn't." I shrugged. "He's just a tool to get Miles to stay away from me. Why is Miles here, anyway?"

"He donated to my campaign in the past. My staff sent him an invite without consulting me." He rocked back on his heels. "Do us both a favor and don't get involved with Knox."

I froze with my hand in the middle of turning the delicate glass doorknob. "Is there something I should know about him?"

"Nothing in particular." He picked at the lint on his charcoal jacket. "I just don't think it's a good idea to get close to anyone right now given what's going on."

I studied him for a moment, trying to determine his motives, but his face was perfectly blank. "Yeah, you're probably right." I opened the door. "Stay here for a few minutes before you join the party again."

He nodded, and I closed the door softly behind me. I sucked in a deep breath through my nose, struggling to calm my frayed nerves.

"Did you find the bathroom?" Knox said, leaning against the wall just outside Derrick's study, his arms folded across his chest.

The fabric of his navy suit jacket pulled across his arms. His blond hair kissed the collar of his crisp white shirt. A lopsided smile inched across his face. His attempt to disarm me didn't work. Beneath his façade of relaxed charm, anger seeped from his pores, and his icy eyes contradicted his phony smile.

My gaze fell away, and I twisted the bracelets on my wrist around and around. I contemplated how to sidestep his question, but in the end, I decided to tell him the truth. I needed his help, and I wouldn't get it if he didn't trust me.

"I never made it to the bathroom. I ran into Derrick Benton, and he wanted to talk to me."

He shot me a damning look. "I thought you didn't know him," he said, enunciating every word with meticulous detail.

"That isn't entirely true, but we don't talk often." He held up his hand to interrupt me, but I ignored him. "Can we save this conversation for the car ride to my place?"

I held my breath, my eyes wide and pleading as I begged him without words to accept my explanation. For now, anyway. I didn't know what I planned to tell him, but it couldn't be the entire truth. My relationship with Miles taught me not to trust easily, and I needed to keep that in the forefront of my mind with Knox unless and until I understood exactly what he wanted from Derrick and me.

Knox shoved his hands through his hair repeatedly. His previously tamed locks stuck out in every direction, and I buried my hands in the folds of my dress to stop myself from smoothing them back in place.

"Fine, but no more lies." Knox's eyes held mine for a beat, and when I couldn't take it any longer, I turned and moved toward the party. Still behind me, Knox cleared his throat pointedly and I glared at him over my shoulder. He held out his hand, wiggling his fingers, a smirk on this face. "Don't you want to hold my hand, sweetheart?"

Right. I'd forgotten about our arrangement. He shoved away from the wall, and I laced my fingers through his. The self-satisfied look on his face didn't escape my attention. "You're enjoying this whole charade quite a bit, aren't you?"

"I am, actually. Miles is playing right into our hands. Have you seen the way he's been looking at you?"

"No." I shivered. "I've been ignoring him."

"Good." He squeezed my hand tighter. "Whatever you're doing is driving him crazy, but I think we can go. I'm done bullshitting for the night."

I smiled at him. "I know what you mean. If I hadn't bumped into Derrick, I would've barricaded myself in the bathroom for twenty minutes to recuperate for round two."

With his hand burning a hole in mine, Knox guided us out of the house and to the front sidewalk. He handed our ticket to the valet.

CHAPTER FIFTEEN

The sky was a gloomy blue-gray. I stared into evening light, taking in the decadent expanse of Derrick's brick-paved driveway. It stretched the length of at least three football fields, looping underneath the white-columned portico of the house and returning to the serene tree-lined street. Flickering gas lit lamps cast a warm glow over the double door entrance. The opulent two-story foyer and the oversized ballroom resembled a hotel more than a private residence. For all its grandeur, something about it unsettled me. Maybe it was the ivy that curled up the side or the twin rows of pines that cast shadows on the driveway like guards ready to pounce on unwilling victims.

A tremor rippled down my spine. Not for the first time since Derrick walked into my life, I noted the disparity between his life and mine. We had the same father, but he had everything handed to him whereas I had to claw my way through life. I didn't resent him for his inherited wealth, his success, or the relative ease of his life, but I couldn't lie. My life would've been so much easier if my father had sprinkled a little fairy dust in my direction. I could've gone to college. My mom might've stuck around to raise Faith and me. I wouldn't have worried when my uncle lost his job. I could've taken all the ballet lessons I wanted.

Sometimes, I wondered why my mom never pressed him for money. But more often, I wondered why he never offered. Unfortunately, I didn't think I'd ever get the answers to those questions. Richard Benton died almost six months ago, and my mom had been gone so long she might as well have been dead too.

I shivered as a puff of cold air curled around my bare arms, goose bumps peppering every inch of exposed skin.

"Are you cold?" Knox said.

"I'll be okay once I get in the car," I answered, rubbing my hands up and down my arms.

"You might freeze to death before then." He hooked his hands around my waist and pulled me against his warm muscled chest. Stunned, I stood motionless. "At a party this size, they need more than one person manning the valet," he said, his warm breath whisked across my hair. My body softened, already traitorously drunk on the feel of his body against mine. What was it about this man?

I nodded absently, each sweeping brush of his thumb against my dress making me breathless in anticipation of his next move. I should've pushed him away, but I was incapable of doing the sensible thing. Voices trickled from the party. The front door opened and closed a few times, but I couldn't concentrate on anything except the tightening of my breasts, the staccato beat of my heart and the rich scent of masculine cologne.

Before I could make sense of his actions or my reactions, he buried his cheek in the curve of my neck. "Did I tell you how much I like this dress? You're beautiful," he whispered, the stubble on his face brushing against my ear. The air hummed with electricity, sharpening the magnetic pull between us.

Temptation surged hard and fast through my veins, and I tipped my head to the side, inviting his touch even though my mind begged me to stop whatever this was before it went too far. God knew, I didn't need to complicate my life any further. In fact, there were thousands of reasons why I shouldn't get involved with Knox, even for a night or a moment. Then he caught my ear between in his teeth and nipped.

"Knox," I muttered. "We shouldn't—" My voice trailed off as his warm lips pressed against the curve of my shoulder, skating up my neck and across my jaw to the corner of my mouth. Thoughts of resisting evaporated like tendrils of smoke in the night.

He transfixed me.

He captivated me.

He held me hostage in a web of desire.

His lips paused near my mouth for a second, waiting for something. A sign? My capitulation? His dilated eyes stared into mine, and my insides knotted uncomfortably. Tension stretched between us, lengthening and thickening with each passing second. At that instant, I would've done anything for him to kiss me. It was all I could think about. My body felt like a time bomb ready to explode.

I opened my mouth to ask for what I needed, and the air tripped in my lungs, a small moan escaping my parted lips. That was all the encouragement he needed. His body shifted closer to mine, our legs tangling and erasing every suggestion of space between us. I didn't know who made the next move, but suddenly our lips fused together like two halves of a whole.

My hands edged up his chest and around his neck, eventually landing in the silken strands of his hair. His lips slanted against mine, and I unlocked my mouth, giving him what he demanded and taking what I wanted. I clung to him, tasting him, exploring him and meeting him stroke for stroke. I melted into him.

"Trinity," he breathed against my mouth, and my heart swelled with warmth. I loved the rumbling sound of my name on his lips.

"Yes?" I answered, sliding one of my hands inside his jacket, twining his striped tie around my wrist.

His hands slipped from my waist, and he stepped back. He cleared his throat. "The car is here."

I blinked away the fog of lust and zeroed in on Knox's blue BMW sedan, idling next to the curb. The valet stood next to the open passenger door, his eyes carefully averted. "Right." I nodded. "I see that."

Ten minutes later, Knox pulled over to the curb on a quiet side street and lowered the volume on his radio to a faint hum. The sudden stop set my already frayed nerves on edge. Neither of us had made a single comment when we got in his car. At some point, he planned to bring up my connection to Derrick, but my mind was stuck on repeat, replaying our kiss so many times I thought my head would explode.

"Look, Trinity, I'm sorry about that kiss. It got out of hand." My stomach rolled, and I clutched my purse to my chest, digging the pads of my fingers into the gold buckle. I didn't like where this was headed. "But when Miles followed us out, I realized he intended to approach you, and I took advantage of the opportunity to make him believe we're together."

Red-hot shame crept up my face. I'd forgotten about his suggestion to pretend we were together. He'd been playing a game to goad Miles, and I got caught up in the moment, romanticizing the kiss. Romanticizing the moment.

"Right, Miles," I finally muttered when the silence threatened to become uncomfortable.

"Good news, though, I think it worked. Did you catch his expression after we got in the car?"

"Um." I licked my lips, then cleared my throat. "Actually, I missed it."

He chuckled. "Too bad. I think you would've enjoyed it."

"Yeah. You're probably right," I mumbled, focusing on the details of the darkened windows in front of me so I wouldn't give in to the insane urge to cry. I felt like a total idiot. Sadly, I didn't want or need another man in my life right now, but the second Knox kissed me I'd been ready to toss my convictions out the window.

He squeezed my upper arm. "Are you okay?"

"Of course," I blurted out. "I was just thinking."

He drummed his fingers on the steering wheel. "Tell me about Benton."

I jerked my head to the side so I could see his face. "What do you want to know?" I asked, stalling for time.

"Everything. I need to understand your motives, and while I believe you're done with Miles, I'm not sure what's going on with Benton."

I chewed my bottom lip. "Why does my relationship with him matter? You told me Lang and Miles were involved in a blackmail scheme. How does Benton fit in the picture?"

"I'm not revealing anything else until I understand the exact extent of your relationship with Benton."

Defeat settled in my bones, and my shoulders sagged. "There's not much to tell. I met him before I moved to D.C. He's helped me out financially on occasion. That's it."

"Did you have an affair with him?"

I snorted. "No. Not even close."

He turned to face me, his back pressing into the driver's side door. "Then start explaining because I'm not interested in playing twenty questions tonight."

"His dad knew my mom. Derrick found me in Texas and helped me relocate to D.C. We've kept in touch over the years, and he's helped me out from time to time. That's it."

He rubbed the back of his neck. "That doesn't

make sense. There has to be more than that." I saw the moment the pieces of the puzzled clicked. His head jerked up, and his blue eyes were glacial. "Please tell me you're not some long lost relation. Are you cousins?"

"He's my half-brother," I whispered, my voice nearly inaudible. My stomach churned with acid. I hated breaking my promise to Derrick, but I didn't see any way around it. I needed Knox's help.

He slammed his hand against the center console. Then he pressed the ignition button and shifted the gearshift into drive.

"Aren't you going to say something?" I asked, tucking my hands under my thighs to stop myself from fidgeting.

Silence engulfed the car as he pulled away from the curb. "Does Miles know?" he asked without looking at me, cold anger wrapping around his words.

"I've never told him, but it's possible." I rubbed my face. "Derrick thinks he knows," I added.

"He's probably right," he said gruffly.

"Are you mad?"

His hooded gaze slanted to me, then returned to the road. "No, but I'm revoking my offer. You can't work with me. This arrangement is over."

Heat rushed to my cheeks, and my mouth felt dry. I needed Knox's help. I was running out of options. I didn't want to disappoint Derrick after everything he had done for me. "Why not?"

"I can't trust you."

"You can," I insisted, moving my head up and down, my heart pounding inside my chest erratically. "Give me a week to prove it."

"Why the fuck would I do that?" he snarled.

"You need my help with Miles," I answered, my stomach clenching painfully.

His car came to a stop in front of my townhome. His head dipped, shrouding his face in the shadows. He looked…dangerous. Ruthless. I didn't know this man.

Uncertainty ghosted down my spine, and I cleared my throat. His icy glare landed on me, and his features appeared more rugged than usual. His cheekbones looked like they were carved in marble, his eyes hooded, his lips sensuous and cruel at the same time.

"No, I really don't. Benton is tangled up in this whole mess, and something tells me you already know that. You're a liability. The best thing you can do is get the hell out of my car and forget you ever met me." He didn't hesitate. He leaned across me and cracked open the door. "Goodnight, Trinity," he gritted out with a steely edge that said he wouldn't change his mind.

I stared at him for a second, looking for a crack in his frosty veneer. His eyes narrowed, and he shook his head slightly, almost warning me not to argue with him.

I sighed in resignation. "Fine. If that's what you want, I won't fight you." I grabbed my keys from my purse. With my head high, I vaulted out of the car and jogged up my front steps, never looking back once.

Screw Miles.

Screw Knox.

I didn't need either of them.

CHAPTER SIXTEEN

Knox

"Fuck." I curled my fingers around the steering wheel until my knuckles whitened. I wanted to hit something. I needed to calm down before I drove home or my car would end up wrapped around a tree.

I fell for her game.

I lost myself in her kiss.

I got sucked into her dark, soulful eyes.

She played me.

"Dammit," I yelled, pounding my hand against the steering wheel.

I knew Trinity had secrets, but it never crossed my mind that she could be Benton's secret half-sister. That not so little revelation screwed up my entire plan. I'd already given her too much information. I had no doubt she'd spend the next half hour spilling everything to Benton. She'd blow my cover. She'd compromise my investigation. And if I didn't walk away from her for good, I knew my life would never be the same.

A little voice inside my head whispered that maybe I wanted things in my life to change. I'd spent my entire life avoiding commitment and believing Archer was the only person I could trust. It made me feel safe. If I avoided romantic entanglements, I could keep my life on track.

Every time things took a turn for the worst, Archer had my back, but now he had Langley. I knew Archer would always be there for me, but it wasn't the same. I didn't begrudge her. She loved my brother, and he loved her. She melted his icy reserve, and I'd never seen him so happy. Watching them made me consider maybe I wanted more than a string of casual flings.

I rubbed my hand down the side of my face, trying to shake off the thought, when a scream pierced the air. Fear surged through my veins. A thud of pain shot through my heart. Without a second thought, I jumped out of my car, not even bothering to fully close the door behind me.

My feet pounded against the pavement. The space between Trinity's townhome and me seemed like a mile instead of twenty feet. When I reached the top of the steps, I ripped my gun from the holster strapped to my ankle and kicked the door open.

The minute I stepped foot inside her townhome, Trinity wrapped her body around mine. I circled one arm around her waist, shoving her behind me, my gun pointed into the dimly lit interior.

"Look, Knox," she said, her voice shaky and her body trembling. Tears streamed down her face.

I scanned the room, and my blood turned into ice. "What the hell," I hissed, my hands clenching into tight fists. An ochre colored cat with a brown tipped tail dangled from a rope strung from the kitchen light fixture. Who the fuck did sick shit like that? "That's your cat, isn't it?" I asked, struggling to keep my voice calm when I wanted to tear apart the person responsible for this.

"Yes. Well, kind of." Her eyes drifted shut, and a visible tremor ran through her body. "It's Max. I found him when I moved to D.C. He kept coming around my place, and eventually he became mine by default."

"Did you touch anything?"

"No." She buried her head in my chest. "I flipped on the light switch next to the front door and tossed my purse on the sofa. That's it." A fractured breath tumbled from her lips. "Somebody killed my cat. What kind of person does that? Why would you hurt a harmless animal?"

"I don't know, babe." I swallowed hard. "Why don't you go sit in my car? I'm going to take a look around, and I'll meet you outside in a few minutes." She didn't need to see this. She shouldn't have to deal with this shit.

"No." Her lips pursed into a tight line. She stepped away from me and my hand slid from her waist. "I'd rather stay here with you. I don't want to be alone."

I heaved out a breath and shoved my gun into the holster at my ankle. "Fine, but stay right here, and don't touch anything."

Not waiting for her answer, I stalked through the

living room, pausing in front of the small round kitchen table. A sweet yet rancid smell coated my nostrils. Breathing through my mouth, I popped open the switchblade on my key chain and raised my arm to cut down her cat. Spotting a folded white piece of paper on the table, I paused mid-reach. Instead, I lowered my hand and flipped open the paper with the tip of my blade. I saw a typewritten note in all caps:

SILENCE IS GOLDEN. SOME SECRETS ARE WORTH KILLING FOR. WHO WILL BE NEXT? WILL YOU LOSE FAITH?

I read the note over and over. My throat dried up, and my hands trembled. Cursing under my breath, I backpedaled a few steps.

"What's it say?" Trinity said, her voice low and hushed.

My lips curled with distaste. "That some secrets are worth killing for."

Her face paled, and she swayed. "Oh my God. Do you think—" Her voice faded, and her chin dipped, resting against her chest.

"Do you trust Benton?"

"Yes." Her head jerked up. "He wouldn't do this. It doesn't make any sense. He found me. He helped me move closer to him. Maybe Miles." She shook her head. "No. I can't see him doing this either. Besides, both of them were at the party. Neither of them would've had the opportunity."

My gut told me whoever killed her cat and left the note wasn't messing around, and despite what

Trinity said, I had no intention of ruling out Benton or Miles. Both of them had an interest in keeping Trinity's connection to Benton a secret. Benton likely wanted to protect his family's reputation and his political career. Miles needed the information as leverage to control Benton's votes in the House of Representatives. I peered around her townhome, looking for more clues. I'd only been inside her place once, but everything appeared to be undisturbed except the cat and the note.

Pulling my phone out of my pocket, I moved to the front door. I needed to think before I acted. I needed evidence, even though my irrational side wanted to put Miles and Benton in a room together and beat the shit out of them until the truth came out. One of them was responsible for this.

"Where are you going?" Trinity asked, her voice sounding lost.

"To make some calls."

Her heels clicked across the floor, and she tugged on the back of my suit jacket. "Don't call the police."

I spun around. "Why not?" I didn't have any intention of involving the police, but I wanted to know her rationale.

Her neck tensed in defiance. "They'll ask me questions about my past. Unless I lie, I'll have to reveal my connection to Derrick, and I promised him I wouldn't do it. I gave him my word. I shouldn't have told you either."

"I think it's obvious your connection to his family is the reason he's being blackmailed." I shoved my phone back into my pocket. "Why do you want to protect this secret? Why does either of you care if people know you're related? Richard Benton is dead. He's been dead for three months or more. Nobody will give a shit that he had an affair over two decades ago."

Her gaze skittered around the room, and she swallowed. "Derrick wants to protect his mother. She doesn't know about me, and according to him, she's in poor heath."

I scoffed. "That's bullshit. Darcey Benton is not sick. Barring an accident, she'll live well into her nineties. She sits on countless boards. She attends charity events every week. She's an avid tennis player. She's in great health."

She stared blankly at the wall for a second, then shrugged. "Maybe you're right. But he doesn't need speculation about me to derail his career, and his family doesn't need their name dragged through the mud over something that happened so long ago."

"Great. I understand why Derrick wants you to keep your relationship secret, which, by the way, is a strong motive for him to threaten you." She held up her hand, but I kept talking, ignoring her. She wanted to protect Derrick, but I didn't like it. He wasn't telling her everything. "And yet, you didn't give me one reason why you cared about keeping your connection secret."

She fisted her hands and her lips thinned in frustration. "I care because Derrick is my brother, and it's what he wants. He's been good to me. He sought me out and encouraged me to move to D.C. He helped me financially when I had nothing." She chewed on her lower lip. "And I don't want anyone to pry into my family or my past. They'll splash my ugly history on the cover of a bunch of magazines. They'll make my mom look like trash. They'll make light of my uncle's criminal history. And Faith…she doesn't need to deal with the gossip. She finally has a life."

I stiffened. "Faith? Who's Faith?"

She sighed softly. "My younger sister. She goes to college in Texas near my hometown. Why?"

I groaned. This was worse than I thought. Her sister's name likely popped up in my investigation of Trinity, but I hadn't committed it to memory. "I think the rest of the note threatened your sister."

Her hand fluttered to the base of her neck. "What do you mean?"

"It said 'Who's next? Will you lose Faith?' The words were in all caps. I didn't realize it referred to a person. I thought it was a bunch of cryptic bullshit."

She gasped as she dropped onto the sofa. "No. No. No," she sobbed over and over again. "I can't let anything happen to Faith. She doesn't have anything to do with this. She's innocent. I need to protect her. She's worked so hard…"

I hunkered down in front of her and pushed back the wisp of hair that had fallen out of her braid. With puffy eyes and red cheeks, she was still one of the most beautiful women I'd ever seen. "I'll send some friends over here to dust for fingerprints and look around. I'll have them clean this up. Do you have somewhere to stay tonight?"

She attempted to wipe the tears from her face. Instead, she managed to smear her mascara halfway down her face. "You can drop me off at The Lux. It's a bar on 9th," she muttered through frozen lips.

I frowned. "I know what it is, but I'm not dumping you at some bar."

Her chest jerked up and down rapidly. "My friend owns the place. I'll wait in her office until closing. Then I'll go home with her. She won't mind."

"No." I rubbed my hands up and down her thighs. I didn't want her to be alone even if it were only for a couple of hours. "That won't work. You're staying with me tonight."

Having her in my space wasn't a good idea. Without a question, if I welcomed her into my home, she'd suck me into a potentially deadly tangled web of lies. That didn't stop me from making the offer. Every cell in my body lit up with the need to protect her.

Her body softened, and she leaned into me, resting her head on the top of my shoulder. Her braid slipped around my back. "You don't have to do that. I know you don't want anything to do with me."

"I wouldn't have offered if I didn't mean it."

"Are you sure?" She lifted her tear stained face. Her coffee-hued eyes glimmered in the dim lighting. "I could go to a hotel or I could stay here."

"This isn't a game, Jones. This is serious. Someone is threatening you. You shouldn't be alone."

I dragged my thumb across her lower lip. She looked fragile, staring at me trustingly with lips that looked so fucking kissable. Damn her for being so pretty. So perfect. She made me want things I didn't think were possible.

"I want you to stay with me." I gave in to the insanity twisting in my chest and brushed a kiss across her forehead, knowing I shouldn't, knowing I was making a big mistake, but I couldn't walk away from her. Not now. Just like that, my decision was made.

"Okay, Knox." She nodded. "But just for tonight."

CHAPTER SEVENTEEN

Trinity

I should've argued with Knox, but I didn't have the energy. I wanted to get away from my house, and agreeing to stay with him for the night was the fastest way to make it happen.

"I need to make some calls," Knox said, squeezing my thigh. "Wait here."

My stomach rolling in nonstop waves, I nodded absently, unable to do anything except stare at Max. I loved that cat. The first morning after I moved into this place, I found Max purring outside my front door. I had tried to get him to go away, but he was stubborn, and he had refused to leave. After a week of him waking me up every morning, I left a bowl of water for him outside my front door. After another week, I added a bowl of food. By the end of the month, Max became my roommate. Now, he'd ended up dead just because he trusted me.

A sob bubbled out of my mouth.

I couldn't take this.

Oh God. Oh God.

How the hell did this happen?

What did I do to deserve this?

I felt like someone had reached inside my chest and squeezed my heart. My rapid-fire breaths echoed in my ears. The edges of my vision blurred then narrowed to a pinprick. My fingers tingled like a thousand ants were crawling inside of my veins. Sweat beaded on my forehead. The lump in my throat tripled in size. Shit. I was having a full-blown panic attack. While they'd been a common occurrence when I moved to D.C., I hadn't experienced one in over a year.

I needed to ground myself in the moment to stop it. I closed my eyes, concentrating on taking slow even breaths. Then I rubbed my hands back and forth on the soft velvet sofa cushions, focusing on the way the plush strands brushed underneath my fingertips. I listened to the deep rumble of Knox's voice as he talked on the phone.

"Trinity." Knox's hands pressed into my shoulders. "Are you okay?"

My fingernails dug into the sofa. "No," I rasped, the word sticking in my throat. "Not even close."

He laced his fingers through mine and yanked me to my feet. "Let's wait outside. The fresh air will make you feel better."

"I'm open to anything," I mumbled, following him out of the door. "I'm losing my mind and my heart feels like it's going to explode inside my chest."

He pulled me into an embrace, tucking my head underneath his chin. Relief seeped through my veins, warming me from the inside out. "It'll be okay. We'll find out who did this."

His hand moved up and down my back in slow, even strokes. I should've walked away from him. This was wrong. He didn't want me in his life. He didn't want anything to do with me. I should've felt the same way. But it felt right to have him soothe me. Comfort me. I didn't want to move away. I wanted him to hold me tighter, prop me up, and support me.

I melted into him, tuning out the world around me. With every brush of his hand, my heart slowed, and my breathing calmed. All I wanted was to move closer to him, crawl inside him, feel him, and be with him. My intuition told me he'd keep me safe. He'd keep my sister safe. I could trust him. I needed to trust someone. I couldn't do this alone, and I wanted him in my corner.

I lifted my head. His gaze was bluer, deeper and more intense than ever before. "I..." The words wouldn't come.

"Shh. You don't need to say anything," he said, his deep, smoky voice dropping low. "We'll figure this out before anything happens to you or Faith."

"Thanks for helping me," I whispered, finally managing to get the words out of my mouth.

The corners of his mouth tipped upward, and he nodded. "You're welcome, Jones."

On impulse, I rose up onto my toes and pressed a kiss against his lips. I wanted to know what it'd feel like to kiss him without any pretenses.

No Miles lurking around the corner.

No need to hide my gun.

Nothing.

Just us.

Just one kiss.

He didn't respond for a heart-cleaving moment, and rejection twisted my insides. I eased backward, but just as quickly one of his hands clamped around my wrist and the other around my waist.

He shook his head, his eyes heavy-lidded. The silhouette of his midnight lashes shaded the sharp angles of his cheekbones. He looked delicious. "Don't stop now," he said, his voice husky. A shiver zipped down my spine

"I…" And there went my ability to speak again.

Pulling me against him, he ducked his head, and before I registered his intent, his lips were on my mouth again. He skimmed his lips over mine.

Once.

My eyes fluttered closed.

Twice.

I moaned softly.

Three times.

My hands curled into the lapels of his jacket.

Then, he stopped.

My eyes popped open. "Can you do that again?"

With twitching lips, he tugged me against his chest. "Later," he whispered next to my ear, deep and with so much promise I thought I'd spontaneously combust. "Right now, I need to talk to these guys, and then we'll leave."

I peeked over his shoulder and saw three men standing on the sidewalk with their backs turned to us. Heat rushed up my neck. "Oh, okay." I glanced at his car. "I'll wait in the car."

***

With our hands threaded together, he guided me into the elevator of his building. He asked me a few questions about Derrick and Miles during the car ride here, but for the most part, we sat together in silence.

"We should know something in a few days," he said.

I nodded, watching the white number on the screen as it ticked upward like a countdown to something. Whether it'd be good or bad, I couldn't say. The fingers of my free hand plucked nervously at the hem of my dress. When the elevator dinged and the doors glided open, the air punched out of my lungs. I reminded myself I was in control and nothing would happen I didn't want.

We walked out of elevator and Knox froze midstride. He released my hand, and I missed the heat. The comfort.

I glanced at him, then in front of us and my heart stumbled inside my chest. A woman with long blonde hair stood next to his door. She instantly sized me up as competition. I didn't wait for her judgment. I looked away. I didn't need a mirror to realize I looked like a mess. Without a doubt, I had mascara smeared down my face. Half of my hair had escaped my braid. My dress was hopelessly wrinkled.

"Brenna, why are you here?" Knox snapped, his jaw tightening.

Her gaze drifted back and forth between Knox and me. "I wanted to talk. I hated the way things ended last time."

He jammed his key into the door, the vein in the side of his neck pulsing. "We've already talked, Brenna. There's nothing left to say. I understand your point of view, and I'm pretty sure you understand mine."

Slowly, she shook her head from side to side. "I wanted to apologize about pushing for more."

Knox pushed the door open. "Is that all?"

Her hands glided up and down her legs. "Um."

Knox braced his hand on the doorjamb and cocked his head toward me. "Because, in case you didn't notice, I have company."

Her hands fluttered to her chest, then she clasped them behind her back. "Are you seeing her now?"

I didn't want to hear his answer regardless of what he said. Our relationship consisted of an unpredictable mix of hostility and desire, and I needed to get away from both of them before the uncomfortable feeling coiling in my gut motivated me to do or say something I'd regret. I dipped under his outstretched arm, darted into his shadowy apartment and flipped on the light switch.

"Knox, I'm going to sleep. It's been a long day. We can talk later." The words scraped like shrapnel across my tongue.

He frowned. "Are you okay?"

"Yes," I answered. My voice was stiff, my smile stiffer.

Clearly, Knox was free to do what he wanted with whomever he wanted. Yet, a small part of me wanted to demand he follow me inside. Resisting the urge, I tried to close the door before he could object. He had other ideas. With the palm of his hand, he kept it propped open. In one seamless move, he bent his head and brushed his mouth warmly against mine in a brief kiss.

"I'll only be a few minutes," he said as he closed the door, leaving me stunned and more than a little confused.

My feelings for him simultaneously frightened and excited me. A small reckless part of me wanted to seize the moment and take whatever Knox offered, even if it only lasted for one night. The logical part of me knew I needed more time to sort out my attraction to him. If Knox were standing in front of me, I had no doubt the reckless side of me would win, but he wasn't and logic won, which meant I couldn't waste a second.

I needed to be asleep by the time Knox returned or at least in a position where I could feign sleep. I ran down the hall and snagged a shirt from his closet. In the hall bathroom, I changed my clothes and finger brushed my teeth while studying my reflection in the mirror. I was a wreck. All semblance of color had disappeared from my face. My makeup made my eyes look like black holes. To top it off, I felt physically ill. Sighing, I scrubbed my face with soap and water and settled onto the living room sofa. I curled in a ball on my side, pulled a throw blanket over my legs and closed my eyes.

By the time I heard the door open twenty minutes later, my heartbeat had slowed, and my eyelids were heavy. His leather-soled shoes shuffled over the hardwood floor, and even with my eyes closed, I could feel him standing at the foot of the sofa, staring at me. I was more aware of him than I'd ever been of another person in my life. It went beyond the remedial training Miles provided me.

He leaned forward, his face moving closer to mine. My heart lurched with panic, swelling and pressing against my lungs, making it hard to suck in air. I curled my hands into fists underneath the blanket. It took all of my willpower not to open my eyes. I wanted this day to end before I compounded the damage to my already turbulent life.

Please don't touch me.

I need to be alone tonight.

I need to think.

As though he heard my unspoken thoughts, he released a weary sigh and walked away. I didn't move a single muscle until I heard the telltale click of the bedroom door.

CHAPTER EIGHTEEN

Knox

Restless. Wired. Pissed off. That's how I felt as I watched the minutes tick by on my alarm clock. I couldn't sleep. From two to five in the morning, I saw every hour; every minute. Thank fuck there wasn't a second hand because I would've ripped my hair out hours ago. At five-thirty, I gave up pretending my eyes would close, and put on my running gear.

When I stepped out the front door of my building, deep purple streaks painted the sky. The crescent moon played hide and seek with the clouds. I loved the early morning when the streets and sidewalks were nearly empty.

Without bothering to stretch, I took off in the direction of the National Mall. Like every other morning, I intended to circle the reflection pool a few times and head home. Halfway there, I took a detour, and twenty minutes later, I found myself on Miles's front doorstep. Rationally, I knew I should stay away from him until I had the evidence to pin the cat incident on him, but my anger overrode my common sense.

After ringing the doorbell nonstop for five minutes, he flung open the door. "What are you doing here?" he growled, his teeth clenched and his eyelid twitching.

A toxic mix of adrenaline and testosterone rushed through my veins. I balled my hands into fists to stop myself from ripping his throat out. "Did you have anything to do with it?"

Folding his arms across his chest, his lips tightened and his brows lowered. "Can you be a little more specific?"

"I'd be happy to." My chest heaving both from anger and jogging, I leaned forward until my face was inches from his. "Did you kill Trinity's cat, string it up over her kitchen table, and leave a note threatening her sister?"

His eyes narrowed. "I didn't touch her cat, and I don't give a shit about her sister. I've never met her."

"Did you have someone kill her cat?" I asked, rephrasing the question. Miles talked in circles.

"My people take their orders from me."

The air around us dropped twenty degrees. I squared my shoulders and rolled my neck, struggling to release the tension curling in my muscles like a wind-up toy. As much as I wanted to convince myself otherwise, beating the shit out of Miles wouldn't help the situation. "Is that a yes?" I asked.

He raised his eyebrows. "No, it's not." He

shrugged. "I won't lie. I don't like that she's using you to get back at me, but I don't want to hurt her. I don't need to. She'll be back with me soon enough."

My brows snapped together. "What's that supposed to mean?"

"She's toying with you to make me jealous. I don't like it, but if it's what she has to do to end up back together with me, I won't stand in her way."

Rage surged through me, and before I could think twice about my actions, my fist connected with his jaw. His head whipped to the side. Blood trickled from the corner of his mouth.

He backpedaled, cupping the side of his face. "What the fuck was that about?" he groused.

I rubbed the knuckles of my right hand down my thigh. "That's for being an asshole. That's for interfering with my investigation. That's for treating Trinity like shit. She's done with you."

He smirked. "You've known her for a couple of weeks now. Is that about right?"

"What does that have to do with anything?"

"It means that you don't know anything about her or our relationship."

My gaze swept down his body and back up again. "She's told me all that I need to know. All that matters."

"Sure, you can keep telling yourself that." He rolled his eyes. "One way or another, she'll be back. I'm just biding my time until I reel her back in."

I cocked an eyebrow. "Are you planning to blackmail her with Benton?"

An uneasy look flashed across his face, but he

hid it quickly. "What do you know about Benton?"

My mouth curled into a humorless smile. "Just what Trinity told me. Is there anything else you want to add?"

"Trinity wouldn't tell you anything. She doesn't confide in people unless she trusts them."

I rocked back on my heels and snorted. "Well, I guess that means she trusts me. Not you."

A sound of muffled anger slid though his clenched teeth. "You're bluffing. You don't know anything."

I arched my eyebrow. "Keep telling yourself that, but it's only a matter of time before I have all the evidence I need to put you behind bars, and I plan to make your life damn inconvenient until I succeed."

He folded his arms across his chest and barked out an uneasy laugh. "Go ahead and try. I don't have anything to hide. I'm not worried."

I glanced at my watch. "Then you're a fucking idiot," I growled as I backed down the front steps of his home. I wanted to get back to my place before Trinity took off. We needed to talk. I was done playing games with her. I wanted her, and I was done pretending otherwise.

CHAPTER NINETEEN

Trinity

Knox strolled in the front door with his polished, loose-hipped gait and a lopsided grin on his face. His navy jogging pants hung low from his narrow hips, and his white shirt clung to his shoulders and chest like a second skin.

He grabbed an icepack from the freezer, molded it around his hand and sat down next to me at the kitchen counter.

His hooded stare raked up and down my body with an unnerving intensity. "That's quite a shirt. You look good in it," he said, his eyes flashing with amusement.

I smoothed the front. "I'm glad you like it."

"How are you feeling today?" he asked, studying me closely.

"Better." I pointed at his hand. "What happened to you?"

He leaned back in the chair, hooking his sneaker-clad foot around the leg of my stool. "I paid Miles a visit this morning, and we didn't exactly see eye to eye."

I reached for my cup of coffee and swirled the dark brown liquid. "Jesus, Knox. What did you do?" I said through a reluctant laugh.

He brushed his hand across the top of my head. "We disagreed on a few matters, and I tried to persuade him to change his mind."

I ripped the icepack from his hand. His knuckles were puffy and red. "By hitting him?"

He lifted one shoulder and dropped it like he didn't have a care in the world. "He pissed me off, so I did what I had to do."

"And what did that get you?"

He chuckled. "Nothing, but I won't lie, I enjoyed it. A lot." He rested his uninjured hand on top of mine, his eyes distant. "I didn't like the way he was talking about you, and I don't trust him. I never have."

I shifted to the edge of the barstool until my face was level with his. I lowered my voice. "Did he admit he had something to do with last night?"

"No." He shook his head. "But I didn't expect him to admit to anything. I wanted to evaluate his reaction both to seeing you with me last night and when I told him what happened to your cat."

I tried to ease my hand out from underneath his, but he tightened his hold. "I don't remember asking you to confront him. In fact, I don't remember asking for your assistance. You helped me with—" I cleared my throat, battling the tears building behind my eyes. "Max. You let me stay here last night, and for both of those things, I thank you, but I don't expect anything else."

"Did you already change your mind? Because I'm pretty sure you wanted something more from me last night." He released his hand from mine and dropped it into his lap. "Or are you telling me I misinterpreted your words?"

"Answer something for me," I said, tugging on the bottom of the shirt I borrowed from Knox. Unless I wanted to put on my cocktail dress, I didn't have any other options when I woke up this morning. "What did that woman want last night?"

He sucked his lower lip into his mouth. "She wanted more than I was willing to give her."

I adjusted the rubber band in my hair, and it snapped. My hair spilled down my back. "What wouldn't you give her?"

He leaned forward, sweeping one arm along the counter and the other along the back of my barstool. "A relationship. I thought it was pretty obvious."

I wrinkled my nose. I didn't need to hear the details to know Knox was probably worse than Miles in the commitment department. I should stop this conversation in its tracks, but part of me needed to hear the words so I didn't keep secretly longing for something between us. "Are you adverse to a relationship with her…or with anyone?"

He tapped his fingers on the table. "For the most part, I avoid anything serious." He glanced to the side. "Relationships aren't easy in our line of work. Too many secrets. Too many late nights. Too many unexplainable exits and absences."

"Was she upset?"

He shrugged. "She wanted me to reconsider, but

I told her another woman snared my attention, and I wanted to pursue her."

My heart clenched. "Where's this woman?"

"I guess it's my lucky day because she's conveniently located right in front of me," he teased, his lips quirking into a crooked grin that lit up his entire face.

Flames shot up my cheeks. "So that's the whole story? There's no ex-wife hovering in the wings?" I tapped my chin with two fingers. "Or a wounded little boy who needs his ego stroked by a variety of women to make himself feel better?"

He slid me off the barstool, positioning me between his legs, and I smelled soap, outdoors, and man. "Definitely no ex-wife or ex-girlfriend."

I grinned, angling my head to the side. "So you're the wounded boy? How sad," I mocked.

His hands closed around my waist, pulling me flush against the hard planes of his chest. The feel of his thumbs as they drew circles on my belly went to my head like a shot of tequila.

"I wouldn't call myself wounded, but I wouldn't object to being nursed a little," he murmured, his voice deep, the corner of his eyes crinkling playfully. His calloused thumb scraped across my lips. I felt that touch all the way down to my toes.

My heart jumped inside of my chest, and my lashes fluttered. "By me or by anyone?" I replied, my voice low and breathy.

His hands twisted in the fabric of my shirt and from the cocky smile on his face, he knew how much he affected me. "Just you, Jones."

I breathed a sigh of relief and surrender. There

were over a dozen good reasons, all of them ready to roll off the tip of my tongue, why I shouldn't get involved with Knox Black. But just like every other time he touched me, I couldn't bring myself to care about any of them. His undeniable strength and vitality seduced me like a siren's song.

His attention dipped to my mouth, and his fingers curled around the back of my head, tangling in my hair. Our eyes locked and he didn't make a move for a fraction of a second. Our lips hovered inches apart. My exhalations became his inhalations. My desire fed his desire.

I skimmed the palm of my hand up his chest, inviting him to continue. He didn't have any trouble interpreting my message. His lips grazed the corner of my mouth, then moved to the sensitive skin beneath my ear. Goose bumps kissed my arms.

He flicked open the buttons of my shirt and parted the white material, exposing me from my neck to the top of my black lace panties. His fingertips trailed along my collarbone down to my breasts, moving lower and lower with every intoxicating swirl. His hand seared me. Branded me. Worshiped me.

When he reached the lace waistline of my panties, my insides clenched and liquid heat pooled between my thighs. A moan tumbled from my mouth, and his pupils dilated, the black core swelling until they nearly eclipsed the clear blue of his irises. Temptation and lust swirled in the air, hot and heavy. Any thought of stopping evaporated like a puddle in the desert.

"Trinity?" he said. His breath felt like velvet

caressing my skin.

Arching my neck, my eyelids fluttered closed in invitation. "Yes."

"Let's go to my room."

I nodded, desire clogging my throat.

He scooped me up, wrapping my legs around his waist and carried me to the bedroom. I didn't murmur a single word of protest because I wanted to live in the present, untethered from everything and everyone.

My cat.

Derrick.

Miles.

My job.

My past.

My future.

And something told me Knox could help me with that.

I clung to him as he lay me down on the bed, his body pinning mine against the white, puffy cloud of bedding. The bright morning sunlight streamed through the long rectangular window that stretched the entire length of the far wall, bathing us in a golden light that felt almost magical.

My hands dove under the hem of his shirt, painting streaks of desire on every sinful contour. His breathing turned rapid and urgent, and his lips crashed against mine. In less than an instant, his tongue thrust between my lips, claiming me. Owning me.

I reached between us and shoved his pants and boxer briefs down his hips. I clawed at his shirt, ripping it over his head and tossing it on the floor.

He toyed with my panties, shoving them to the side, not even bothering to remove them before his fingers plunged inside me. An uncontrolled tremble rushed through my body.

"Knox, please," I said, the words blurring into incoherent syllables.

I clutched his shoulders, my nails digging into his skin. With his lips next to my ear, he told me how much he craved me from the minute he saw me. He told me I was the most beautiful woman he'd ever seen. He mumbled dirty, filthy things that should've made me blush, but instead they made me desperate for him; desperate for this.

My body hummed with need, every nerve buzzing on high alert. Bowing off the bed, I rocked against the heel of his hand, hungry for more. His free hand palmed my breast, rolling one nipple between his thumb and forefinger, then the other. More dirty words and just like that, I tumbled over the edge, the pleasure so surreal it bordered on pain. His lips melded against mine, drinking my moans and groans into my mouth like he wanted to save them for later.

He yanked his fingers out of me. "Dammit, Trinity," he hissed. "This is going too fast. I can't wait any longer."

He rolled off me and sat on the edge of the bed. I pushed onto my elbows, watching him pull a condom from the top drawer of the nightstand. His brows pulled together as he ripped it open and rolled it down his shaft. When he finished, his blue eyes laser-focused on me, sweeping over my body with enough heat to set me on fire.

"These need to go," he said, his voice smoky, deep and perfect. He yanked my panties down my legs. Seconds later, he braced his body over mine, his hands bracketing my head, his triceps bulging. He slid his erection back and forth over my entrance, testing and teasing with the heavy press of his hard length. Greedy anticipation vibrated in my core, and I realized I had never felt so impatient for any other man; certainly not Miles or the two other men who came before him. With them, I was going through the motions, taking the obligatory next step in the relationship.

Before the thought could take root, he plunged inside of me.

In.

Out.

Back in again with skilled movements that had me riding the edge to oblivion faster than I wanted to admit.

His body pressed into mine, and his hands drifted to my hips, angling my pelvis so perfectly. Too perfectly. I circled my legs around his waist, wanting him deeper. Fire knotted low in my belly, spreading and growing stronger with every thrust.

"God, you feel good. Too good," he whispered.

I nodded because words weren't possible. My climax shimmered infuriatingly near, but too far out of my reach. I moaned in frustration, and as if he could read my mind, his hand snaked between us and strummed against my clit. Like magic, my muscles tensed. I gritted my teeth. My pulsed jackhammered inside of my chest. My blood raced through my veins. My sex clenched. I arched off the bed, chanting his name like a benediction. One jagged thrust later, he followed me over, a string of curses interspersed with a guttural groan flowing from his parted lips.

Minutes ticked by and neither of us uttered a word. I clung to him, not wanting to let go. Not wanting the moment to end. I didn't want to face reality and the problems and uncertainties hanging over my life like a thundercloud.

Too soon, he rolled onto his side and wrapped his body around mine, our legs tangling together. His hands explored my body, but without the heat of a few minutes ago. My eyes felt heavy, and I yawned, the sleepless night catching up with me.

"Are you tired?" he asked, his fingertips drawing circles on my belly.

"Yeah." I rotated onto my other hip so I could see his face, my hair rustling on the pillow. "I didn't sleep very well last night or the night before that. I've been a wreck between worrying about my brother and my job." I poked him in the chest. "And you didn't help matters. I didn't know what you wanted from me." I pursed my lips. "I still don't know."

The corner of his eyes crinkled in amusement. "I'm a man of mystery."

"Something like that." I rolled my eyes. "Seriously, though, where do we go from here?" The weight of my words hit my stomach as if I'd swallowed acid.

He blew out a breath. "Honestly, Trinity." He sat up, his legs dangling over the side of the bed and his back to me. "I don't know."

Flames shot up my face, and I was thankful he didn't turn around to look at me. With shaky hands, I buttoned my shirt. "I'm not trying to push for a relationship if that's what you're worried about. Last night you all but kicked me out of your car and life, and now this happened." I waved my hand in the air.

He pulled his shirt over his head and yanked on his pants. He dropped his head for a second, clearly contemplating what to say to me. Then he stood and pressed a kiss to the top of my head. "Why don't you take a nap and I'll run over to your house and pick up your things. I think it'd be safer for you to stay here for a couple of days."

I shook my head. "That's it. That's all you have to say?"

He raked his hands through his blond hair and it stuck out in a dozen different angles. He looked boyish, adorable even. Damn him for being…him.

"Yes."

"Look." I sat up, my gaze settling on the strong column of his throat because I didn't want him to see the disappointment etched on my face. "Just take me home. I don't want this to be awkward, and I sure as hell don't want you to feel obligated to let me stay at your house."

"Relax, Trinity," he murmured, pressing a hand on my shoulder. "I don't have all the answers right now, and neither do you. Let's process this for more than a few minutes, and we'll go from there."

I stared at the bedding, feeling foolish. He was right. I didn't know what I wanted from him either. "All right."

"Good." He grinned. "I'll be back in an hour or so. There's plenty of food in the kitchen. Help yourself to whatever you want."

"I will."

He cupped my face as he kissed my mouth hard. I wrapped my arms around his neck, my fingers twitching to yank him back into bed and start all over. No thinking. Just touching.

He untangled my arms from his neck, a maddening closed-lipped smile on his face. "I bet you will." He walked to the entrance of the bedroom. He grabbed a pair of aviator sunglasses from the top of the dresser and slid them on his face, pausing for a moment. "And try to refrain from rifling through my files again."

"Jerk." I threw a pillow at him, but he dodged it without difficulty.

His deep laugh echoed down the hallway.

CHAPTER TWENTY

Knox

I pulled into a parking place down the street from Trinity's townhome, and I checked my phone. There were two messages from Archer, demanding I call him immediately.

"Hey, Archer. It's me," I said.

"Finally," Archer growled. "I was about to file a missing person's report. You haven't returned my phone calls for a week."

"Yeah. Yeah," I said, feeling like a major asshole. I glanced out of the rear window of my car to see if I was being followed. "I'm busy. If you haven't noticed, I have two fucking jobs, and my boss for one of those is a real piece of work. He's always riding my ass like I don't have anything else to do."

He chuckled. "I assume you're referring to me."

"If the shoe fits…" I answered, swinging my legs out of my car, then pushing the door shut behind me.

"Don't think I didn't notice that you still haven't

finished that security update for Black Investments."

I switched my phone to the other ear and pumped a couple of quarters into the meter. "I haven't forgotten about it, but it will probably be a few weeks before I can wrap it up."

"What's going on?"

I glanced up and down the street. "You know how these things go, Archer. I can't talk about it on the phone. In fact, I shouldn't tell you anything, ever, but I wouldn't mind bouncing some ideas off you."

My brother was one of the smartest people I'd ever met. He was a wizard with numbers and had an uncanny ability to see through the bullshit. Jack was a good business partner. We understood each other, and I respected his work ethic. He respected me, but I would never trust anyone as much as I trusted Archer. I had idolized him for as long as I could remember. That would never change.

He was only a couple of years older than me, but if it weren't for him, I probably wouldn't have survived past my fifth birthday. To put it mildly, my mom was a shitty parent who took her role as a victim seriously. Until the last year of her life, she used vodka to cope with the fallout from one self-created disaster after another. I'd spent my entire childhood and most of my adult life hating her. Resenting her. She stripped away my innocence and subjected me to the ugly side of life before I could even walk. Her neglect lingered over me like a thunderstorm my entire life.

"Then you're in luck. Langley and I are in D.C.

for a couple of days. I made reservations for the three us at that sushi place in my building at seven-thirty."

Even though he and Langley moved to L.A. a year ago, Archer still owned his plush condo in the Four Seasons Hotel. He did everything but hold a gun to my head to get me to buy the place from him, but I didn't want it. I made good money, especially in the past year or two, but nothing like Archer. It didn't hurt that his fiancée had a healthy trust fund too.

I leaned my hip against a bike rack, crossing my ankles. "I don't know, Archer. I am swimming in a pile of shit right now. Can we meet for coffee tomorrow?"

He didn't answer for a second, and I could imagine the look of disapproval splashed all over his face. "Langley will be disappointed."

I grinned and shoved my free hand into my pocket. "Just Langley, not you? I think you've got that backward."

Langley was a beautiful and talented woman. My brother looked at her like she had created the universe. And for that, I loved her, but I wasn't deluded enough to think she returned the sentiment. She tolerated me. She invited me to their home for the holidays, but I'd always gotten the distinct impression that I made her uncomfortable, nervous even.

Archer sighed. "Dinner was Langley's idea. She wants to get to know you better. I want the two most important people in my life to know each other and be friends. What's so bad about that?"

Guilt swirled in my gut. Archer was right. I needed to make more of an effort with Langley. She wasn't going anywhere, and I didn't want her to. She softened all my brother's hard edges.

"Fine." I rubbed a hand down the side of my face. "Can you change the reservation to four people? I'd like to bring someone."

"A woman?"

"Yes." I curled my hand around the icy metal of the bike rack.

"Seriously?" Archer said, drawing out the word.

"Yes." I rolled my eyes. "Don't sound so surprised. I'm not a complete asshole."

"What happened to the three and done rule?" he asked.

In the past, I kept my relationships short and sweet. I didn't want any commitments. I didn't want anyone encroaching on my freedom, and I sure as hell didn't want anyone telling me what to do. Since I met Trinity, none of that seemed important. I wanted her in my life and in my space. The thought of her walking out of my life in a couple of days or a couple of weeks hit me like a punch to the gut. Unfortunately, I didn't know if I could trust her. My gut said yes, but I'd be the first to admit lust clouded my judgment when it came to her.

"Yeah, well, this woman is different," I responded, my voice gruff.

"If she successfully navigated the three date Knox obstacle course, then she is different."

"We haven't been on three dates. In fact, we've barely made it through one," I confessed.

Archer didn't respond for a prolonged beat. I

heard paper shuffling in the background, indicating he was working. He was always working. Less now that he lived with Langley, but he still put in ten-hour days.

"Ah, I suspect there's a story there."

"Probably. I don't know." I pushed away from the bike rack and started walking down the street, maneuvering between people. "It's complicated."

Archer chuckled. "It always is. How'd you meet her?"

I snorted. "She pointed a gun at me, and basically threatened to kill me."

"Wait. You're kidding, right?"

"No."

"Not exactly a fairytale beginning."

"No. Certainly not," I agreed, pausing in front of Trinity's house. "But neither was your first encounter with Langley."

Last year, Archer concocted a plan to destroy Senator Wharton, his biological father. He used Senator Wharton's stepdaughter, Langley, to make it happen. Somehow, they ended up falling in love and getting a sickeningly sweet happily ever after.

"Maybe not, but no guns were involved."

"Right, the guns came later," I said dryly, referring to Senator Wharton's attempt on Langley's life that landed him in prison.

"It's water under the bridge." He cleared his throat. "So, does this woman you're not really dating have a name?"

"Trinity. Trinity Jones," I said, pulling her key out of my pocket and stuffing it in the keyhole.

"I can't wait to meet her."

"I bet."

"It's true, but do me a favor and tell her to keep her guns at home."

A laugh burst from my lips. "I'll do my best."

CHAPTER TWENTY-ONE

Trinity

Knox and I walked into Leslie's bar. It was pitch black with a few well-placed spotlights and the glowing onyx bar. Music pulsed through the speakers. People laughed a little too loud. Perfume mixed with sweat and alcohol tickled my nose. I was glad I didn't have to work in a bar any longer. I enjoyed the tips, but I hated the late nights.

We were supposed to meet Knox's brother and his fiancée in an hour and a half. Meeting Knox's family seemed premature. He told me he wanted to take things one step at a time and see what happened. I agreed because I had enough complications in my life, but there was something about Knox that made me crave more. Every time he walked into the room or his gaze landed on me, my stomach tightened in wistful longing.

Knox wrapped his arm around my waist,

molding me to the side of his body. "Don't be nervous about meeting my brother or his fiancée. They don't bite."

"I'm not." I laughed lightly, trying to cover the blatant lie.

"Then why were you fidgeting with the clasp on your bracelet the entire drive here?" Knox grinned as he pulled out a stool at a high round table near the bar and gestured to the seat.

I dropped my purse on the table and perched on the edge of the stool, being careful not to flash my panties to the entire bar. If I had more time to get ready, I would've insisted Knox stop at my townhome to get a different dress than the one he'd grabbed from my closet.

The red satin dress had a deep V neckline and a razor cut back that exposed the sides of my waist. The bottom flared into an A-line silhouette, but it stopped well above the middle of my thigh. Leslie talked me into buying it a couple of months ago, but I could never bring myself to wear it in public. Its lack of coverage made me decidedly uncomfortable.

"I don't know." I glanced over to the bar and raised my hand to catch Leslie's attention. Her nearly white hair darted back and forth behind the bar as she moved from customer to customer. "Maybe I'm more worried about you meeting my friend." I tugged on the front of his deep blue dress shirt and lowered my voice. "She might bite."

One side of his mouth tilted upward in a dazzling grin, then he pressed a kiss to the corner of my mouth. My heart fluttered violently against my ribcage. Without fail, every time he directed his attention on me, I felt like a flimsy piece of paper caught up in the tornado that was Knox Black. "I trust you to keep me safe."

"Well, hello," Leslie said, her hands on her hips and her eyes narrowed in disapproval.

"Hey, Leslie," I said, reluctantly dropping my hand from Knox's shirt.

Knox held out his hand. "I'm Knox Black. It's good to finally meet Trinity's best friend. I've heard so much about you."

He exaggerated, but I didn't call him on it. I'd mentioned a few things about Leslie on the car ride over, but nothing too revealing.

Leslie flipped her white blonde hair over her shoulder as she eyed Knox's hand for a suspended second. "It's nice to meet you, Knox Black." She shook his offered hand. "Trinity hasn't breathed a single word about you until an hour ago, but I won't hold that against you…yet."

Knox arched one eyebrow. "Good to know."

"So, how did you two meet?" Leslie probed.

Knox smiled down at me, the front of his thighs brushing against my knees. My stomach clenched. "Why don't you tell her about our first meeting?"

I rolled my eyes. "Knox is a business associate. We met at a party, and now we're…" I licked my lower lip. "Hanging out."

His lips twitched, but he quickly wiped his hand across his lower jaw to hide his amusement. "That sounds about right."

Leslie planted her hands on her hips, a scowl scrunching up her dainty facial features. "Are you related to Archer Black?"

He folded his arms across his chest, and cocked an eyebrow. "Yes. He's my brother. Why do you ask?"

"No reason." She shrugged. "I was just curious."

"Trinity," he said, focusing on me again. "Do you want something to drink?"

"Sure. I'd love a vodka on the rocks with two limes."

"I'll be back in a few minutes." He brushed his fingertips down my arm. A simple feather-soft touch and warmth bloomed in my chest.

I watched him until he disappeared into the crowd. I shook my head. "We're going to dinner with his brother and his fiancée tonight. How do you know Archer Black?"

Leslie sat on the stool adjacent to me. "I don't know him personally, but everyone knows who Archer Black is." Her brows scrunched together. "Don't you?"

"The name sounds familiar, but I can't place it." Leslie's eyebrows scaled her forehead. "Why do I get the feeling you're about to lecture me about something?"

"Archer Black is a self-made millionaire or billionaire. I don't know which, but he has a shitload of money and connections. His fiancée is Langley Mayer, former stepdaughter to the now imprisoned Senator Wharton and if you read the tabloids—"

"I don't," I snapped, shifting in my seat. The long gold chain around my neck swung between my breasts like a pendulum. I didn't want to know all of this background information. I was nervous enough without feeling socially and financially inferior.

"Well, she's the next 'It' girl in Hollywood." She lifted and dropped one shoulder nonchalantly. "Which isn't surprising considering she is the daughter of Rick Mayer."

"Great, so I'm going out to dinner with a man who could buy me a million times over and Hollywood royalty."

She nodded. "Pretty much, but that's not why I'm pissed at you."

"What do you mean?"

She propped both of her elbows on the smooth metal tabletop and leaned forward. "Didn't you learn your lesson with Miles?"

"Apparently not, but I have a feeling you're about to enlighten me."

She tapped her fingers on my hand. "Don't shit where you eat, Trinity."

I giggled. "I try not to. That sounds unhygienic," I said, purposely misunderstanding her declaration.

"You know what I mean. Don't date your boss or business associates. It's messy."

My hand fell into my lap with an exasperated sigh. "I know. It's stupid, but this thing with Knox has a short shelf life. Both the job and the relationship are temporary. I'm using him, and he's using me. It's not a secret. We both know how this is going to end." My insides contorted painfully. I didn't want there to be any truth in my words.

She eyed me suspiciously. I erased all emotion from my face, hoping she couldn't read between the lines and realize I was already in too deep with Knox. I shared things with him—real things that I'd never told another living soul. Palpable, newfound intimacy sizzled in the air every time he looked at me.

"Okay." She lowered her voice. "Just don't get lost in him and forget who you are."

I nodded, breaking eye contact with her to look for Knox, but mostly to regroup. "Don't worry about me. It's not going to happen."

Even to my ears, it sounded like a lie. Luckily, she didn't call me out because I couldn't defend my actions or my behavior. It didn't make sense. I should have run away from him instead of toward him.

CHAPTER TWENTY-TWO

Knox

I glanced at my wristwatch. Archer and Langley were late. Normally, I wouldn't mind, but Trinity looked like she would come out of her skin if they didn't show up soon. I rested my arm over her shoulder and slid her body closer to me.

"Hey, don't worry about Archer or Langley. They'll like you."

She swallowed, her gaze fixed on the clear glass bubble chandelier near the entrance. "I know I'm over-thinking the whole thing, but once Leslie gave me the lowdown on them, I'm feeling a little overwhelmed."

"That's why I didn't say anything."

She frowned. "That's not comforting."

I swiped a hand down my face and exhaled. "Look, I won't lie, most people are intimidated by Archer. On the surface, he seems hard and calculating, but underneath he's a softy. And Langley…" I paused, considering my words as I twirled her dark hair around my finger. "She's one of the genuinely nicest people I've ever met. Before she started acting, she was a physical therapist. She cares about people. She's going to jump through hoops to make sure you feel comfortable."

She swiped the tips of her fingers along the crisp white tablecloth. "If you say so," she said, noncommittally.

"I know so." I glanced at the floor to ceiling glass windows running the entire length of the front of the restaurant. "But you can judge for yourself. They're here."

Her leg bounced up and down on the oyster colored cushion. "I can't believe you talked me into this. You owe me."

"I'll think of a way to repay you."

I stood to greet Archer and Langley. His characteristic grin spread across his face. "Hey, little brother," he said, wrapping me in a one-armed hug. "Sorry we're late. We had some stuff to take care of."

"Yeah, I bet you did," I said, pulling away. "Langley, good to see you." I kissed her cheek. As usual, Langley had a big grin on her face. Her golden hair hung in loose waves, nearly reaching the middle of her back.

"Hi, I'm Langley," she said, holding her hand out to Trinity.

"Trinity," she responded, shaking Langley's hand.

"And this is Archer." Langley elbowed my

brother.

"Right. I'm Archer." He squeezed Trinity's arm. "Sorry if I'm acting strange. I'm shocked my brother actually showed up with someone."

Trinity's gaze flicked to me, then back to Archer. "Oh, really? Why is that?"

He shrugged, then settled into the booth next to Langley. "Let's just say this is the first time I've met anyone he's dating since high school. He normally keeps them well hidden or he kicks them out of his life so fast they're not worth mentioning."

"There's no need to scare away my date," I said, laughing humorlessly. For the first time in memory, I wanted a woman to stick around. I liked her. I enjoyed her company. On top of all that, I needed her to unravel Miles's blackmail scheme. "Let's move on to another topic."

"Fine. We'll talk about something else," Archer said, his eyes narrowing fractionally as he placed his napkin in his lap. "Trinity," he said, redirecting the conversation. "Are you from D.C.?"

***

Archer cornered me coming out of the restroom after dinner.

"Hey," he said, slapping me on the shoulder. "You seem a little stressed."

I shoved my hands into my pockets. "Like I said on the phone, I have a lot going on right now."

"Trinity seems a little guarded, but nice. She's a nice change from your usual type."

"Yeah." I glanced at the table and passed the

palm of my hand over my face. Langley's hands swirled in front of her as she explained something to Trinity. "I'm not sure if it's going to lead to anything serious, but I like her too."

He leaned his hip against the wall and folded his arms across his chest. "So what's her real story?"

Stepping back, I shook my head slightly. "I'm not sure. I only know bits and pieces."

His eyebrows jumped up his forehead. "Seriously, Knox, you hired her without running a full background investigation on her? I know she's attractive, but you've never fallen victim to a pretty face before."

I pinched the bridge of my nose. "Of course I did a background check. It came back pretty clean, which is amazing considering the big ass skeleton in her closet."

"You. Me. Langley. We all have skeletons in our closets. It's not always a bad thing." His voice was soft, gentle even. "Our history doesn't define us."

"I get that, Archer. I really do, but I can't decide what side she's on."

He smirked. "That sounds familiar."

I chuckled. "It does." Archer hadn't been sure he could trust Langley, and it blew up in his face. She forgave him, but she made him wallow in misery first. "Listen, I can't share the details, but I'm investigating a blackmail scheme that involves coercing members of the House of Representatives to change their votes. One of the Representatives being blackmailed is her half-brother, and the secret they're using to blackmail him with is her."

Archer whistled as he ran his hand through his

almost black hair. "That's not good."

I snorted. "I realize that."

"There's only one way to stop the whole mess in its tracks."

"I know," I said, wary.

Nodding, he shoved away from the wall, one of his hands lingering in the pocket of his pants. "They have to put together a joint press release spilling the details of her identity."

"Jesus, Archer, I can't ask her to do that. She doesn't want the connection revealed and neither does he. It won't happen."

"Do you want my advice?"

"Not really," I lied. I trusted Archer. He was one smart son of a bitch. He never steered me wrong.

"Too bad because I'm going to give it to you anyway." He followed me down the hall, the soles of his shoes clipping over the tiled floor. "Ask her to do it. See how she responds."

I yanked on the cuffs of my shirt. "And if she refuses?"

"Then you have your answer."

I glanced at him from the corner of my eyes. "What answer?"

"You want to know whose side she's on? Where her loyalties lie? If she doesn't ask him, she's on his side, and you can't trust her."

"Yeah, you're probably right," I agreed, my gut clenching uneasily. I didn't want to let Trinity go, but I might not have a choice. Benton and I were on different sides. He betrayed the trust of his constituents by folding under the weight of a blackmail scheme instead of coming clean. I was hired to expose him and anyone else involved.

"Don't look so distressed. She might surprise you."

I tugged on the collar of my shirt. "We'll see."

CHAPTER TWENTY-THREE

Trinity

"So what did you think of Langley and my brother?" Knox asked as he handed me a glass of wine.

I flopped down onto one of Knox's tan sofas and tucked my legs underneath me. "I don't think they hated me. That's a good sign, right?"

"Yes. I think they liked you a lot." Knox sat in the sofa directly across from me, bracing his elbows on his thighs, his eyebrows lifted. "I want to talk you about something."

"Oh." I twirled my wineglass by the stem, watching the golden liquid swirl in circles. "Is it bad?"

"Not bad." He shook his head. "The opposite really. I had an idea on how to defuse this situation with Benton."

I took a sip of the white wine, not even paying

attention to the flavor as it rolled down my suddenly dry throat. "What's your idea?" I said, turning my attention to the window. Clouds hovered near the darkening horizon, cloaking the skyline.

He scrutinized me with a gentle smile on his face. "If Benton acknowledges you as his half-sister publicly, this entire situation will go away. The blackmailer won't have any power over Benton, and it will keep both you and Faith safe."

"There has to be another way." Even as I said it, I didn't know if it were true. What he said made sense.

He rose and sauntered across the room. He braced one hand against the sliding glass door. "There might be, but it will take considerably more time than we have given the threat against your sister."

"I'll just leave. I'll move across the country, change my name, and start over. If I disappeared, nobody could prove anything. It'd be unsubstantiated rumors."

"That won't help anything and you know it," he said wearily.

My stomach plummeted, and I nodded even though he wasn't looking at me. He was right. Even if I disappeared, I'd still exist and that was probably enough to blackmail Derrick. "I know."

He turned to face me, the murky light shading the lower half of his face. "Nothing good will happen by keeping this secret." He shrugged as he moved closer to me. "The story will play out in the tabloids and on a few websites, but it will fade quickly enough. Richard Benton died six months ago. Nobody will care and given the type of scandals floating around these days, having an illegitimate child is pretty tame in comparison."

"Yeah, you're probably right." I swallowed. "I should talk to him and see what he thinks."

"That's a good idea."

"Am I going to regret this?"

"It's possible," he whispered. "But I'll do everything to make sure you don't get hurt in the process." He reached out and tucked a strand of hair behind my ear, and my heart fluttered inside my chest. "Archer will help, too. He has a lot of sway with the news media, and we'll hire you your own P.R. team, so someone is looking out for your interests, not just Benton's."

Tears burned the back of my eyes and I dropped my gaze. "Thank you. That would be great. I don't know how I'll pay for it, but I'll make it work."

"I'll help with the cost." He cupped my face, cradling it, looking down at me. Everything faded away, the sadness, the loneliness, and the fear of the future. In that instant, only the two of us existed. There was no barrier, no cool suspicion in his clear eyes. Just trust, understanding and acceptance.

I pulled my phone out of my pocket.

His lips tightened. "What are you doing?"

"I'm calling Derrick."

"You don't have to do it right now. It can wait until morning."

"No." I whipped my head back and forth. "I need to, otherwise I'll chicken out. I don't want him to hate me."

This wasn't the first time I wanted to bring this

up with Derrick. But somehow the thought had never translated into an actual conversation.

He flashed a white smile. "He's not going to hate you for suggesting it. Nobody could hate you."

My eyebrows lifted. "I hope you're right." I didn't want to lose my brother. I could count my family members on one hand. The thought of losing one of the three who were still part of my life made me sick to my stomach.

I pressed the green button to call him.

He squeezed my shoulder, his eyes boring into mine. "Do you want me to give you some space? I can go into the other room or wait in the lobby of my building."

"No," I rasped, listening to the first ring. "I need you to stay."

"Hi, Trinity. What's going on? I didn't think I'd hear from you until Monday."

"I have an idea I want to run by you," I blurted out, my knee bouncing up and down.

I heard a door shut. "It's getting late. Ellen and I just got home from a dinner party. Can it wait a couple of days?"

I shook my head. "No. It can't. Some stuff has happened since the last time we talked." He didn't answer. "Derrick? Are you still there?"

"Yes." He sighed. "What happened?"

Knox squeezed my neck lightly and nodded for me to continue.

I licked my lips. "When I got home after your party, my cat..." I closed my eyes and swallowed back the sob begging to surface. "Somebody killed my cat and left a threatening note, warning me to keep my silence."

"I'm sorry, Trinity. Did you call the police?"

"No. I didn't think it was a good idea for either of us."

He blew out a long, drawn out breath. "That's good. I'll have some people look into it. I can have some people test the note for fingerprints and—"

"No. I'll take care of it," I interrupted. "That's not why I called. I think…" I paused, taking time to get my words right. "I think we should consider coming clean." I cleared my throat, hesitating to say anything else. His silence prompted me to continue. "I don't know. We could make some announcement or do an interview so it's controlled. I'm sure you have people who could spin the story to your advantage. We could focus on your effort to welcome me into the family instead of the affair."

"You seriously want me to voluntarily air my family's dirty laundry for everyone to comment on like we're part of some trashy reality T.V. show? Do you even understand what this would do to my family? You might have been raised by a felon with no morals, but that's not how I do things," he said, his voice arctic. His cold words hit me like a slap to the face. I couldn't speak for a second.

Derrick never indicated he knew much about my uncle, but apparently, he had done his homework. My uncle was arrested more than once in his late teens and early twenties, but he cleaned up his act after my mom disappeared. I have no doubt he walked on the wrong side of the law on occasion, but he worked as a car mechanic for as long I had known him. He may have been laid off from time to time, but he always found something.

"This isn't just about *your* family. Your decisions affect me too. You may want to ride this to the end and deny everything, but I'm not going to put my friends and family in danger because you want to protect the Benton name."

Sometimes you don't know if you've made the right decision until after you've made it. And this was undeniably one of those times. His words made me think he never cared about protecting me.

"I didn't mean it that way," he said softly.

"Of course you meant it that way. You've told me countless times you didn't want to turn the lives of your family upside down, but never once have you expressed any concern about how this has impacted me. You didn't have to hunt me down or tell me the truth. You could've left me alone and no one would've known."

"My dad asked me to find you."

My mouth dropped open in shock. "What? You never told me that."

"He'd just been diagnosed with cancer when he asked me to find you and make sure you were okay."

I squeezed the phone, and Knox's hands curled around my shoulders, but I couldn't look at him. I knew he could hear the conversation and I didn't want to see his reaction. I rubbed the dull ache inside of my chest.

"I don't get it. Don't you think that piece of information was important? Why didn't you say anything before?" My voice sounded like I'd swallowed a mouthful of glass.

Derrick's breathing turned heavy, then he sighed. "I couldn't. Look, I realize this is a touchy subject for both of us. I think it'd be better if we had this conversation in person. I don't want to fight with you."

"Yeah. Okay. You're probably right." I was too shell-shocked to object, and part of me wanted to end this conversation as fast as possible so I could process everything. "But I still want you to consider what I said about coming clean."

"I'll text you on Monday and we'll schedule a time to meet for lunch in the near future. We can talk about everything then."

"Sure," I said, my voice breaking mid-word.

I disconnected my phone and tossed it on the coffee table. Without saying a word, I stood and warily slipped past Knox. For some reason, knowing my biological father sent Derrick to find me hurt. I couldn't help wondering if I missed out on an opportunity to meet him. Derrick never suggested it, but I didn't know the details of his illness. He was diagnosed with brain cancer around the time Derrick found me and he died almost six months ago.

"Are you okay?" Knox asked, following me down the hall.

Instead of answering, I shook my head. I didn't have anything to say and didn't want to hear anything Knox might say just yet.

CHAPTER TWENTY-FOUR

"Where are you going?" Knox asked, his shoes clipping over the hardwood.

I opened the bathroom door. "I'm getting ready for bed. I'm beat. It's been a long day." With trembling hands, I dug through my cosmetic bag, searching for my brush.

He leaned his hip against the doorjamb. "Do you want to talk?"

I scoffed. "No. I think I'll pass." I couldn't have a heart to heart right now. I'd lose my mind.

He sighed. "Let me help you."

He grabbed the brush from my hand. With slow even strokes, he worked the bristles through my tangled hair. He grabbed an elastic band from the counter and arranged my hair into a ponytail.

"Who taught you how to brush a woman's hair?" I asked, my gaze meeting his in the mirror.

"I used to do it for my mom when I was a kid."

I smiled, imagining a miniature Knox combing

his mom's hair. "That was nice."

"Not really. I had to do it for her when she was too drunk to do it herself."

"Oh." I frowned. "She was an alcoholic?"

"That and a lot of other not so good stuff." He tossed the brush on the top of my bag. "I don't want to talk about her."

My heart squeezed. "I know how you feel. I hate talking about my mom. She was a great mom, but then one day she disappeared without a trace, and we never heard anything from her again." I swallowed. "I don't even know if she's alive."

He spun me around. "I'm sorry, Trinity. It must be hard wondering if she's out there somewhere—"

I pressed my finger to his lips and shook my head. "I don't want to talk about that either. Not tonight, anyway."

He pulled me flush against his body. His warm soothing embrace made me feel like he could keep all the monsters away. "Agreed," he murmured.

Lifting onto my tiptoes, I closed my arms around his neck. Then he kissed me slowly, seducing me with his mouth, his lips, his teeth, and his tongue. I'd never been kissed with such committed focus. Within seconds, he had me convinced that nothing mattered in the world except that kiss. I gave myself up to it, following his lead and kissing him back with a single-minded intensity that quickly ignited into a frenzy.

I reached for his shirt, my fingers fumbling to shove the tiny buttons through the holes. He clamped his hand around my wrist and I felt his smile against my lips. "It's not a race. We have all night," he said, his voice deep and hypnotic.

He lifted me, wrapping my legs around his waist. I closed my eyes, relaxing into him. I pressed my lips to his neck, and he groaned. He shifted me closer to him, eliminating every suggestion of space.

My back hit the mattress, and he moved over me. He caught my hands in one of his, holding them above my head. His tongue glided against mine, tamer now than in the bathroom. My heart knocked against my breastbone, eagerly awaiting his next move.

He reached under the hem of my dress, his warm hands clashing with my icy skin, setting me on fire one brush of his fingers at a time. I was so distracted by his touch, my mind barely registered the moment he slid my dress over my head.

I snuck a hand between our bodies and palmed him through his black pants, needing evidence I affected him as much as he affected me. He groaned as I circled the outline of his erection, his eyes squeezing closed.

"Jesus, Trinity." His voice was rough and needy, and a shiver rippled through my body.

He ripped his shirt over his head. I worked open his belt, then his button and zipper, needing to touch every inch of him. He pushed my hands away, shoving his pants and boxer briefs down his legs. He certainly wasn't a stranger to the gym. His chest bulged in all the right places. Unable to stop myself, my fingertips drifted over the silky expanse of his chest. Everything about him was sexy; too sexy. The narrowing of his waist tempted my hands to move lower, but he captured my hands in his again.

"You're moving too fast again," he whispered against my neck.

"But I want to touch you."

He chuckled, his warm breath sending goose bumps spiraling down my arms. "Hold on to the headboard," he said, curling one of my hands, then the other around the wooden slats above the bed. "I want to touch every part of you."

His fingers skimmed the column of my throat to my collarbone. He pushed down one bra strap, then the other. He reached behind me and unclasped my bra, unwrapping me like a present on Christmas morning. A low hum of pleasure pulsed through my veins.

"I like this one. Red looks good against your skin, but I like them better on the floor." He dangled it from his finger and flung it across the room. We watched it fall to the ground. "The same goes for these," he whispered, sliding off the matching panties.

He kissed his way down my body, exploring every curve and indentation with his mouth and his hands. I couldn't breathe. I couldn't move. I couldn't talk. I was his willing prisoner.

Parting my knees, he kneeled between them. "You know what my first thought was when you stormed into Lang's study with your gun drawn?"

"No." My voice was raspy. Needy. I thought I was going to spontaneously combust if he didn't move this forward.

He ducked his head, pressing his lips to the inside of my thigh while his fingers slid against my sex. Wet sounds mingled with my panting breaths. My world narrowed to those to two points of contact, my body vibrating and my teeth chattering.

"I thought you were the most beautiful woman I'd ever seen." He lifted his head, his gaze searing into me. "And I still think you are."

I opened my mouth to respond, but the words got caught in my throat when his finger circled my clit.

"I wanted to throw you over my shoulder and carry you out of there," he said, his lips painting a line from my leg to my core.

"Knox," I mumbled, but it sounded more like a whimper than a word.

"Would you have let me?" he asked.

"God, yes." My hips bowed and my sex clenched greedily for more.

He ran his tongue along my entrance in one decadent lick that made my head spin. Then he pulled my clit into his mouth, sucking tenderly. My head rolled to the side accompanied by a long drawn out moan. Lacking the strength to keep my eyes open, they fluttered closed, the muscles in my thighs trembling. Meaningless syllables spilled from my lips. I buried my hands in his hair, moving against him as my insides coiled tighter and tighter with every swipe of his tongue. Then he added a finger. Maybe two. I didn't know. I was beyond caring. One delicious swirl, and I shattered into a thousand tiny pieces.

Instead of rolling off me, his mouth explored his way up my body, showering me with hot and wet kisses.

My navel.

My breasts.

My neck.

Behind my ear.

By the time he reached my mouth, he had somehow put on a condom. He clamped his hands around the bottom of my ribcage and pinned my hips against the mattress. In one skilled thrust, he pushed a few inches inside of me, his eyes never leaving mine. I rocked my hips, but he held me steady, refusing to move until he was ready.

Dipping his head, he pulled my nipple into his mouth, caressing the aching bud, and a little mewl of surprise slipped from my parted lips. My heart pounded so hard it felt as if it would fly out of my chest any second. I rubbed my hands up and down the backs of his legs, feeling his solid, ropey muscles beneath the coarseness of his hair.

I arched, pushing him deeper inside of me. I couldn't get enough. He moved with controlled little thrusts that ignited spasms of devastatingly intense pleasure. My body stiffened, already straining for a second release.

Sweat beaded on his brow. "So good, Trinity. So good. You're perfect for me." His voice was lazy with desire.

My heart squeezed both in pleasure and terror because his words echoed the ones bouncing around in my head. "I know. I know."

He slid in and out, hitting the perfect spot, coaxing a shuddering moan from my lips. I dug my fingernails into his hips, urging him without words to move faster. Harder. He did exactly that.

Our skin slapping.

Our moans tangling.

Our hands exploring.

Our mouths colliding.

It shouldn't have been so easy to bring me back to the brink again, but within seconds, ecstasy washed over me. I cried out with the force of my release, my body arching and trembling beneath his. My entire body tingled, my nerves fizzing. My lips were numb, and all of it went on and on.

My spasms were still rippling through me when his started. He bucked into me, his head thrown back and his neck corded as he shook and pulsed. A low groan rumbled up from his chest, punctuated with one fierce pump of his pelvis. He collapsed on me, unmoving, his heart thundering against mine. Good God, I was officially addicted to him.

Finally, he raised his head, his hands bracketing the sides of my head, and he stared at me with lucid, thoughtful eyes. "You okay? Was that okay?" he asked, his voice earthy and full of gravel.

"Better than okay," I whispered, uncertainty lacing my words.

Knox's lips glided across mine, and our sweaty skin suctioned together. "I meant what I said."

I smiled as he peeled his body off me, tucking his head next to my neck. Clinging to the moment, I hooked my arm around his body, listening to the tangled thuds of our hearts and the soft whispers of our exhalations.

CHAPTER TWENTY-FIVE

Knox

"Where are you headed?" Trinity asked as she poured water into my coffee maker.

"For a run. Do you want to join me?" The minute the words escaped my mouth, I regretted them. After last night, I needed space and time to clear my head so I could concentrate on my work instead of all the conflicted feelings for Trinity vying for attention inside my head.

Just thinking about it, forced the remnants of panic to the surface.

"Sure." She pressed the on button for the coffee maker and gurgling noises floated through the kitchen. "But we need to stop at my house first. I don't have sneakers here."

My gaze swept down her gray t-shirt and black yoga pants, drinking her in. "Are you ready to go?"

"Yeah." She rolled a rubber band off her wrist

and pulled her hair into a messy ponytail on top of her head. "I'll drink my coffee in the car." She pointed to the twin blue mugs on the white quartz countertop. "Do you want some?"

I crouched down to tie my shoes. "Nah. I'm good."

The minute I stepped over the threshold of Trinity's townhome, I took a reluctant, tentative sniff of the air. Dryness, dust, and the lingering odor of burnt coffee curled into my nose. I flipped on the light, and a pained hiss escaped Trinity's mouth.

My feet were rooted to the floor as I surveyed the scene in front of me. "Fuck. Wait right here," I ordered, without bothering to turn around to see if she listened.

The soles of my shoes crushed over broken glass, coating the floor like confetti. Deep gashes marred every cushion of her once sleek gray sofa. The kitchen chairs were turned upside down creating an unintentional obstacle course. Light spilled from the open refrigerator door. Food was strewn all over the floor.

I picked up a knife and made my way to her bedroom. It wasn't my weapon of choice. If the person who did this were lurking somewhere in the shadows with a gun, I'd be fucked. I couldn't count the number of times I had chastised Archer for failing to carry a gun at all times, and now I was guilty of the same damn mistake.

The bedroom and bathroom didn't fair any better than the rest of her house. The drawers were ripped out of the dresser. Clothes tangled with the bedding on the floor, covering the hardwood with splashes of color. The mattress rested on its side against the white bed frame.

"Oh my God," Trinity whispered behind me.

I spun around. "I told you to stay put."

Tears streamed from her red-rimmed eyes. Her hands trembled as she pulled at the hem of her shirt, stretching it to the middle of her thighs. "I know, but I couldn't just stand there. I had to see the damage for myself."

"Come here, Trinity," I whispered, pulling her into my arms.

"Why? I don't get it. I haven't done anything to deserve this. First my cat and now this," she murmured into the crook of my neck, her hands curling like claws into my shirt. "But you know what?" She pulled away from me, her eyes slanted into angry slits. "I'm fucking sick of this. I've worked hard to get where I am. Sure, Derrick helped me out here and there, but I've made it where I am by working hard and not giving up. If whoever did this thinks I'm going to roll over and play dead because they trashed my apartment and killed my cat, they're wrong. Because now I'm pissed. Really pissed."

She stomped across the room, kicking shoes and clothing out of her path. "I didn't care about any of this shit anyway. I can get new clothes and furniture." She flung open her closet door. Standing on her tiptoes, she reached onto the top shelf and retrieved a round white and gold music box with a delicate ballerina in a sea green tutu on the top.

A sigh slipped from her lips, and she swiped the back of her hand underneath her eyes, erasing all the evidence of her tears.

"Is that yours?"

"My mom gave it to me the last time I saw her," she answered, cranking the dial on the bottom. A playful melody floated through the air.

"What's that song?" I asked, taking a few tentative steps closer to her.

"It's the Sugar Plum Fairy by Tchaikovsky."

"The Nutcracker?" I said, absently.

"Yeah." She sniffed.

I moved even closer to her. "Was it a birthday present?"

"No." She ran the tip of her finger down the side of the ballerina. "She gave it to me to celebrate a better future. She claimed our lives were going to change after that day. Unfortunately, they did, but they changed for the worse. She never came home from work. My uncle was left to raise us. He wasn't an awful person, but was caught up in his own life and he didn't pay much attention to us. We ran free."

My brows knitted together. "You never found out what happened to her?"

"No. My uncle filed a missing person's report, or at least he said he did, but nothing ever came of it. I tried to find her using some of Miles's resources, but every lead has been a dead end."

She stuffed the music box into her oversized black tote bag. "I should probably throw it away. It's kind of childish, and it holds more ugly than good memories." She bowed her head, a sad smile on her face. "I had this silly dream that I'd grow up to be a prima ballerina. When my mom disappeared, so did my dreams. My uncle refused to enroll me in another ballet class. He didn't continue my mom's tradition of taking us to The Nutcracker every Christmas. Basically, my life was never the same." She closed her eyes. "It's like she left this giant gaping wound in my chest and it's never gone away. Not completely. Sometimes it fades. Then something reminds me of her and the pain is fresh again, just like it happened yesterday instead of over a decade ago."

"I know." I brushed my fingers along her cheek. "Archer and I couldn't run away from our mom fast enough. We lost touch with her for a while. I was in the military. Archer was busy taking over the world one investment at a time, and she was doing God knows what. I always thought I'd get a call that she drank herself to death, but it didn't happen that way."

She tilted her head to the side. "How did she die?"

I shifted on my feet. "A few months before she died, she called me to tell me she was sober and had a job. She wanted us to visit her. Archer went. I didn't."

She pursed her lips. "Why not?"

"I can't really explain it. It was more of a gut reaction. I had mentally written her off from the time I graduated from high school. I considered her part of my past, and I wanted to keep her there."

"Do you regret not seeing her?"

"Yeah." I rolled my shoulders back. "More often than not, she was checked out and unable to see the horror of what she was doing to her kids. On occasion, I'll have a good memory of her when she wasn't drunk or stoned, but then I remember all the crap she put us through on a daily basis, and the hate takes over again."

"I feel the same tug of war with my mom."

I cleared my throat. "The police thought she had committed suicide."

She frowned. "She didn't?"

"No." I swallowed. I hated talking about this. "Senator Wharton paid someone to kill her. I'm sure you heard about it in the news."

Her eyebrows darted up her forehead. "Wow. And Archer and Langley…"

I shook my head. "What he did doesn't have anything to do with them. Besides, he's in jail. They're satisfied with the way things turned out."

"Are you?"

I shoved my hands deep into my pockets and tipped my head to the ceiling. "Yeah. I wished I would've made that trip with Archer to see my mom, but I wasn't ready. She caused a lot of damage—" Trinity opened her mouth to interrupt and I held up my hand. "I'm not saying she deserved what he did. She didn't, but she wasn't a good person. Sure, she had demons. We all do, but she never faced them. Instead, she used them as an excuse to justify her bad behavior."

I flexed my jaw. "She left us home alone for days without food or money. She'd come home drunk, and I'd hold her hair while she vomited." My gut churned, the long-buried memories torturing me with razor-like claws. I closed my eyes briefly, forcing them away. "There's more. Worse stuff. But

I think you get the gist of it."

She averted her eyes. "Yeah. My uncle drank too much sometimes and pretty much ignored my sister and me. He left us alone a lot, but I was already ten when my mom disappeared."

I rubbed my hands together. "Did you find your sneakers?"

She pointed to the gray sneakers on the closet floor. "They're right there, but I can't go. I need to figure out what to do with this mess."

"Nope." I grabbed her sneakers. "We're going to take that run we talked about. Then we're going to stop by my office. After that, we'll talk about what we're going to do."

Her gaze drifted over the mess. "You're right." She tugged the shoes out of my hand. "Let's blow off some steam."

CHAPTER TWENTY-SIX

Trinity

After we had left my place, we jogged the pebbled pavement paths of the National Mall until I begged him to stop. We sat on a small black lacquered bench for an hour eating ridiculously fattening pastries, drinking coffee, watching the tourists and joggers, and swapping childhood stories. When we couldn't ignore reality any longer, we made our way to his office. It didn't escape my attention that Knox kept glancing over his shoulder the entire morning, most likely checking to see if we were being followed.

"Is your partner going to be here?" I asked as he punched a code into the keypad and pressed his index finger to the screen.

"Probably. He rarely goes home."

"Why's that?"

The lock clicked and Knox pushed open the door.

"He and his wife don't get along. He uses work to escape her. I think that's the reason he pushed us to set up shop in an apartment rather than a traditional office."

"I heard that," a voice called from inside.

Knox placed his hand on the small of my back, guiding me inside. "If I cared if you heard, I would've whispered."

The studio apartment had one large room with a wall of windows on one side and a small kitchen tucked in the corner on the adjacent wall. A large rectangular table took center stage in the middle of the room. Computers and other tech equipment covered half of the surface.

A man with medium brown hair and similarly colored eyes sat in front of a computer monitor, his legs spread wide. His hair stuck up in every direction, and a least a week's worth of stubble covered the lower half of his face.

Knox gestured to me. "Jack, this is Trinity Jones."

Jack pushed away from the desk and stood. He had a bulky muscular build with broad shoulders. "Nice to meet you." He stuck out his hand and I shook it.

"Likewise," I said.

Jack turned his attention to Knox. "I didn't realize you planned to come into the office today."

Knox tossed a white bag of pastries on the table. "I didn't, but I wanted to check on those reports from Trinity's apartment."

Jack slid a blue file folder across the table. "There's nothing to see. Everything came back clean. The only fingerprints in the entire apartment were yours and Trinity's.

Knox flipped open the folder and trailed his finger down a piece of paper. "They must've wiped down her entire townhome."

Jack nodded. "Yeah. That's what I thought."

Knox tossed the folder on the table. "What about the encrypted files from Lang's computer? Have you had any luck with those?"

Jack's gaze swept down my body. Anger vibrated from his pores. "I'll fill you in later." He cocked his head in my direction and breathed a sigh of irritation. "When she's not around."

Knox bent at the waist, his palms flat on the top of the table. "You can talk in front of Trinity."

My throat tightened, I backpedaled a few steps. "It's not a big deal. I can wait in the hall."

Knox straightened and folded his arms across his chest. "It is a big deal. You're assisting me on the case. Jack knows that."

"No. I don't know that." Jack popped out of his chair, the wheels scraping across the floor. "I don't know what sort of game you're playing right now, Knox, but this shit has to stop. You may be the majority owner, but my life is on the line here, too."

Knox's eyes glittered. "What are you trying to say?"

"That I don't trust her, and the last time we talked, you didn't trust her either. Dammit, Knox." He banged his hand on the table and released a sharp breath. "Just because you're fucking her doesn't mean she's not going to shove a knife in your back the second you're not looking."

Wow. This guy was a jackass. "Look." I held up my hands and took a few steps back. "I'm not getting in the middle of this."

"No." Knox clamped his hand around my wrist, but he didn't break eye contact with Jack. "You're not going anywhere. Jack, apologize to Trinity."

"I'm not going to apologize. I'm your partner. She's just some chick you're using to get information to crack this case. The exact same case that I didn't want anything to do with six months ago, but no." Jack waved his arms wildly in the air. "You overruled me, and now we have Miles Knightly crawling up our asses, and you're defending some woman with a murky as hell background. What next?"

Anger pulsed through my veins and I yanked my wrist out of his hold. I didn't know who I wanted to hit first—Knox or Jack. "What the hell, Knox? You're using me? That's what you told him? Is that what this is about?"

Shaking his head, he reached for me again, but I swatted his hand away.

"Listen, Trinity." He shoved his hands through his hair. "There's nothing nefarious going on. I never misled you. I told you exactly—"

I couldn't do this right now, especially not with Jack in the peanut gallery. I needed space. I needed air. I needed to think. I felt like I was on a never-ending merry-go-round ride.

"You know what?" I swallowed, but my throat was too dry to complete the motion. "I don't want to hear your fumbling explanations and I don't want his apology. He's entitled to his opinion, but just for the record," I said, pointing my finger at Jack, and then Knox. "I have a lot more at stake than either one of you. I'm the one with the dead cat and the trashed townhome. In fact, since I met Knox, my life has imploded. I should be questioning whether I should trust both of you, not the other way around." I inhaled through my nose as I shook my head. Instead of calming me, it was like throwing gasoline on a campfire. "So screw you. Screw both of you. I don't need this, and I sure as hell don't need either of you to figure this out. You two can sit in here and play footsie and whisper secrets. I'm done."

Pivoting on my heel, I stormed out, so mad I thought flames had to be shooting out of my eyes. I rushed past the elevator to the fire exit door. I flung open the heavy gray-hued door and it crashed into the concrete wall with a satisfying thud. The slapping of my sneakers against the metal stairs competed for attention with the loud drumming of my heart.

Grabbing the tubular railing, I whipped my body around the landing like a slingshot. One more flight of stairs and I reached out for the door handle leading away from Knox and his asshole partner. Just as I cracked the seal of the door, strong arms circled my waist. I hadn't even realized he followed me. The sound of our lungs sucking in air filled the dimly lit stairwell. Seconds passed. Weighted. Heavy. Then I snapped.

"Get your hands off me," I said through gritted teeth. I dug my fingernails into his forearms and donkey kicked backward, hitting him in the shin.

"Dammit, Trinity. Just calm down for a second."

"Calm down?" I screamed. "Are you serious right now? You want me to calm down when my life is coming apart at the seams and I just found out the one person I thought I could trust was using me?" I dragged the palm of my hand down the side of my face. "Sorry. That's not happening."

Months of self-defense training wasted, he grabbed my wrists and locked them in one hand behind my back, easily overpowering me.

His teeth scraped along my earlobe. "I'm sorry about what happened in there. Jack was being an ass. I should've talked to him before I brought you here. I should've explained what was going on."

I shouldn't be so angry. Knox hadn't made a single promise to me about the future. In fact, he hadn't once brought up the subject of what might happen once this case ended. Stupidly, I deliberately steered clear of the topic of us, not wanting to come across as too pushy or needy.

I leaned my forehead against the door. "Are you using me? Is that what this is about? Is that why you're letting me stay at your house, sleep in your bed, and…and…" I couldn't bring myself to finish that thought because if he used sex as a tool to persuade me to help him, I'd lose my mind.

I'd done a lot of dumb things in my life like trusting Miles, moving to D.C. with no job and less than a hundred dollars in my pocket, but I couldn't forgive myself for falling for Knox if I was nothing more than a pawn to him.

He spun me around, his deep blue eyes stormy. "I haven't lied to you. I told you I wanted to make Miles jealous so he'd pursue you. We discussed this.

You agreed to help me get information. I don't understand why you're mad."

I shoved my hands between our bodies and tried to push him away. He didn't budge. "You're right. I agreed to your plan, but I thought we'd moved beyond that. I thought we were…" My stomach plummeted as the memory of encountering that woman waiting for Knox outside his door floated through my mind. She wanted more, too. He said he couldn't give her more. I slapped a hand over my mouth to stop myself from saying anything further. I'd embarrassed myself enough already.

His eyes softened and he pulled my hand away from mouth. He pressed his lips against mine, but it was too much. I turned my head to the side and squeezed my eyes shut. Maybe he'd take pity on me and leave me alone.

He framed my face with his hands, and I reluctantly pried my eyes open. "I know what you're thinking and you're wrong." He leaned his forehead against mine and groaned. "I care about you. I respect you."

A sharp pain sliced through me. As stupid as it seemed, I believed him. My heart told me he would never intentionally hurt me, but I wanted more than respect from him. I wanted his heart because I had a sneaking suspicion he was well on the way to claiming mine.

I jammed my hands into my pockets, so many thoughts on the tip of my tongue, but I feared if I opened my mouth I'd cry, and I refused to cry in front of him. I had too much pride for that, and I sure as hell wouldn't scream or beg him for more than he wanted to give me. After all, I was a big girl, which meant I had to take responsibility for my actions. Leslie had warned me not to push the boundaries of my professional relationship with Knox, but I did it anyway.

"Are you going to say anything?" he asked, staring at me with a look so intense that goose bumps showered my arms.

I shrugged, hoping if I feigned indifference, he'd walk away. I was at the end of my rope, and the sooner he walked away, the sooner I could freak out. "There's nothing to say. We made a deal, and I got caught up in the fantasy of us. I misinterpreted your actions." I pressed a hand to my breastbone, trying to will away the growing ache. "At this point, I think it'd be best to make a clean break and part ways. I don't feel comfortable with this anymore."

"No." His voice cracked like a whip rushing through the air and his blue eyes blazed with anger.

I cocked my chin to the side. "No? What do you mean, no?"

CHAPTER TWENTY-SEVEN

Knox

I took a deep breath, searching her angry eyes, darker now than they had ever been, and I was fucking tongue-tied. I shoved my hand into my hair, tugging at the roots like a deranged lunatic. I didn't have any experience coaxing a woman to stay in my life. I never cared enough to bother. As a rule, I kept my relationships with women casual, uncommitted and uncomplicated. I didn't censor my comments or consider how my actions would affect a woman because I never wanted a future with any of them, so nothing I said or did mattered in the grand scheme of things.

But Trinity had crashed into my life and here I was—chasing her down the stairs with a hundred half-baked apologies on the tip of my tongue, my heart thumping erratically inside of my chest from something other than exertion.

Logically, I should've let her walk away. We already had too much baggage and we'd only met a month ago. And we'd only been together for the last two weeks of that. Wanting her the way I did considering everything going on in our lives seemed crazy. But that hadn't stopped me from rearranging my entire life to make room for her.

I moved her into my house.

I just punched Jack, my fucking best friend and partner, in the face.

I introduced her to my brother.

I made nice with her friend who wanted to rip my dick off the moment she met me.

I did all of that because I wasn't ready to say good-bye to her. It felt wrong. I liked waking up next to her in the morning. In fact, I wouldn't mind seeing her face every morning. In other words, I could see myself keeping her around for the long haul and have the fucking white picket fence and two-point-five kids with her—and that was impossible. I wasn't cut out for that life. My mom had systematically destroyed my belief in other people and love, but I sure as hell could delay the inevitable as long as she'd let me.

I closed my eyes for a second, gathering my thoughts. "It wasn't just about Miles and using you to get information. When I told you I wanted you from the minute I saw you, I was telling the truth. That hasn't changed. I turned my life inside out to fit you into it. I didn't need you to puzzle together the pieces connecting Miles, Benton, and Lang. I used it as an excuse to get what I wanted."

"And what's that?" Her words echoed off the

concrete walls.

"You." I slid the pads of my fingers over her pouting lips.

Her eyes softened and she nodded. "What now? Where does this leave us?"

"That depends on you," I said quietly.

"On me?"

I smiled. "Yeah. What do you want?"

She stared at me for a beat, reluctance etched into her face, then she took a heavy breath. "I want to explore this. Whatever it is," she admitted. "But—"

Not wanting to hear her objections, I kissed her, but it was so much more than a kiss. Every little thing felt more significant and more unforgettable with her. Did she feel the same or was I the only one so wrapped up in us that I couldn't imagine a future without her?

A familiar sensation hummed through my body and every one of my senses zeroed in on her.

Her lemon scent.

Her pouty lower lip.

The delicate curves of her waist.

The way her curves molded against my body.

I groaned. Everything about her fit me perfectly, almost as if she were created for me and me alone.

My hands moved to her waist and I shoved her running pants down her legs. This stairway was seldom used. Even if it had been highly trafficked, I probably wouldn't have cared. She kicked her pants to the side, and I didn't waste a second. My fingers sought and found her wet heat, sliding, teasing and circling. Pleading noises tumbled from her mouth, and she clawed at my pants, jerking them over my hips.

She looked beautiful. Her neck was arched. Her dark hair tumbled down her back in waves. Her cheeks were flushed. Her eyes glowed. Her lips were parted. I wished I could transport us back to my apartment so I had time to explore every inch of her.

I yanked up her shirt and pulled one pink nipple into my mouth, then the other. She swayed and I lifted her, wedging my hips between her long legs. My hands easily spanned her waist, making me realize how incredibly small she was compared to me. I leveraged her weight against the door. Her hands curled around the back of my neck.

My brain told me this was the wrong time. The wrong place. The wrong choice, but damn, everything about Trinity felt so right. I was slipping past the point of no return. Maybe I already had.

Somehow, without even trying, she made me break all my rules, but I didn't care. I wanted to be under her skin, in her heart and in her thoughts. I wanted her to think of me when she closed her eyes at night. I was ready to give her everything.

I aligned my cock with her entrance. "Is this okay?" I whispered next to her ear.

"Yes," she groaned. "I want you."

I didn't wait for clarification. I fused my mouth to hers as I slid inside her, drinking every one of her sexy little moans like a fine glass of wine. I moved in and out, the door rattling with every thrust, announcing what we were doing to anyone nearby. The noise should've compelled me to stop this insanity. My life, my profile, and my job demanded discretion. Right then, I didn't care.

"Every time, Trinity. Every fucking time," I murmured next to her ear.

The pads of my fingers dug into her hips, gripping tight, and I moved a little harder, a little quicker, like we were on a race to the finish line. With her back leveraged against the door, she met me thrust for thrust. Fleetingly, I worried I was being too rough, but her shuddering breaths and incoherent pleas told me otherwise.

Her movements turned jerky and a little frantic, and fuck if I didn't feel a little out of control too. Being with her was raw and honest, and every time I touched her, I fell further under her spell. My arms shook with exertion. My legs burned like the fires of hell. My heart pounded. Sweat dripped down the side of my face.

All too soon, her inner muscles clamped around me. My name tore from her lips and she tossed her head back, exposing the long line of her throat.

I dragged my nose up her neck. "You make me lose my mind, every fucking time," I growled.

Her eyes fluttered open, dilated and dreamy. This woman…

Pleasure snaked down my spine and I cursed under my breath. I couldn't hold on any longer. She felt too good. She smelled too good. One more flex of my hips, and I spiraled over the edge of reason.

Our breaths echoing off the concrete walls, I leaned my forehead against hers for a second. The scent of sex filled the air. When I could move, I released her legs and slipped out of her.

I pushed the loose strands of hair away from her face. She caught my wrist and brought it to her lips. "I'm sorry about that. Normally, stairwells aren't my style."

She laughed as she pulled her pants up her long legs. The sound was low, husky, sexy. It made me want her again.

"It's a first for me, too," she said, a faint blush dusting her cheeks.

"Are we okay? I've never been in a real relationship, but I'm trying."

"Yeah. We're good. I'm sorry I ran away like that. I'm just—"

My phone rang in my pocket, the sound amplifying in the tight space. I yanked my pants over my hips. "I need to get that. It's Jack's ringtone. He's probably wondering what happened to me."

She sucked her lower lip into her mouth and averted her gaze.

"Hey," I whispered, framing her face with my hands. "Don't worry about Jack. I'll take care of him. He isn't normally so confrontational."

She raised her eyebrows. "I won't take that shit from him again."

"Noted." I reached into my pocket to retrieve my phone. "What's going on?" I said.

"Are you still around?" Jack asked, his words clipped.

I traced the collar of Trinity's shirt with my finger. Her answering smile was tentative and sweet. "Yeah."

"Well, get your ass back in here. I just hit the

mother lode."

I snapped my hand away from her and rubbed it down the side of my face. "What are you talking about?"

"I figured out how to open the encrypted files. God, you aren't going to believe the crazy stuff he kept on his computer. Either he wanted to get caught or he is dumb as fuck."

My heart rate skyrocketed. "We'll be there in a minute, but you need to cut the bullshit with Trinity. I trust her."

"Why are you pushing this? Why do you care about her?" he asked. "We have everything we need. We don't need her. Cut the ties."

"No," I barked, my gaze colliding with hers.

"Oh, shit," he muttered. "You can't be serious. Please tell me she's not under your skin. Please tell me you're not in love with this woman."

I sighed. I wasn't having this conversation right now. I couldn't explain my feelings for Trinity. I wanted to be around her. I wanted to touch her, talk to her. I craved her, but I didn't know what any of it meant.

"When have I ever steered you wrong? You know me. You know I don't take unnecessary risks." I squeezed Trinity's arm. "I trust Trinity with my life."

"Fine." He blew out a breath. "If you trust her, I'll go along with this. For now, but I'm keeping my eyes open. You're more than my partner. You're my best friend. You've stood by me through all this shit with my wife and respected my choices. I'll do the same for you."

"Thanks, man. We'll be up in a couple of minutes." I disconnected the phone and threaded my fingers through hers. "We have to go back in there. Jack opened Lang's encrypted files."

Trinity cleared her throat. "I gathered that."

My mouth pulled wide, unable to take my eyes off her bee-stung lips. "This is a good thing. It could be the break we need."

The tight lines between her eyebrows softened. "Okay, let's do this, but if he's a jerk—"

I kissed her forehead. "You have my permission to kick him in the balls," I deadpanned.

CHAPTER TWENTY-EIGHT

"Remind me why you wanted to do this in the middle of the night?" Trinity grumbled, her hands stuffed deep into the pockets of her black trench coat. "I'm freezing my ass off."

Trinity, Jack and I stood on the back patio under a wood trellis of Representative Lang's house dressed in black from head to toe.

I squeezed her hand but released it just as quickly. "It's better this way. Miles's surveillance team leaves after Lang turns off his bedroom light."

Her gaze drifted to the balcony on the right side of the second story, and she wiped her palms down her thighs. "Well, they're off," she whispered.

Jack's finger repeatedly stabbed at the screen of his phone. "You don't have to whisper, Trinity. He knows we're coming."

Trinity shot a glare in Jack's direction, but he didn't lift his head. Jack hadn't warmed to Trinity in the last few days, but he kept his thoughts to himself, and for the most part, he behaved civilly toward her.

A circle of light bobbed inside of the house from the second story to the main level. At least Lang had enough common sense to use a flashlight instead of turning on every light in the house, broadcasting our arrival to everyone.

"The alarm and his security cameras have been disabled," Jack said, his eyes still glued to his phone.

Quick, rapid pants of air escaped from Trinity's mouth.

I slid my hand inside the holster strapped around my waist and pulled out a gun. "Here he comes."

Lang cracked open the glass door, his gaze sweeping over the three of us, and then landing on my gun. Sighing, he opened it wider. "You don't need that. I'm not armed."

I cocked one eyebrow but otherwise ignored his comment. I wasn't taking any chances. We backed Lang into the corner, and in my experience, people never responded well when they didn't have options.

I waved my gun at Lang. "Jack, pat him down."

Lang rolled his eyes and propped his hands behind his head. "At least ask the girl to do it. It'll be more enjoyable that way. I saw the way she kissed you in my study at the fundraiser last month. Did you bring her along as entertainment?"

My jaw flexed and my hand tightened around the gun, but I ignored the taunt.

Trinity didn't. She laughed. "I don't think you'd enjoy my type of entertainment. I hear your tastes are a little younger, much more helpless, and of the male variety."

Jack chuckled as his hands moved systematically up and down each of Lang's jean-clad legs. Then he came to his feet, patting the palms of his hands over the front and back of Lang's light gray cashmere sweater.

Lang's mouth snapped closed, his eyes narrowing and the vein on the side of his neck throbbing. "That's all a bunch of bullshit."

"Save it for someone who wants to listen to your lies. I'm not interested," I said.

"He's not armed." Jack yanked Lang's hands from the back of his head and clasped them in one hand behind Lang's back. He grabbed a pair of handcuffs from his pocket and secured them around Lang's wrists.

Lang spun around. "What the hell is this about?"

"We're not taking any chances." I handed Trinity the car keys. "Jones, you're driving."

"Where are we going?" Lang asked, the corners of his eyes wrinkling.

"We're taking a little drive." Jack ripped his gun from his holster and pressed it to the back of Lang's head. "Now, walk."

Lang jerked his head from side to side, his eyes wide with panic. "You're fucking crazy. I agreed to talk to you from the comfort of my house. I didn't agree to be carted around in the back of your car like a fucking criminal. I'm an elected official. You need to treat me with respect."

"Are you done with your tantrum?" I drawled, sounding bored.

"No. I changed my mind. I'm not doing this." He

pulled his arms a few inches away from his lower back, and the metal of the handcuffs rattled. "Take these things off."

I sighed wearily. "Do you want to go over your options again? Because I assure you what's happening now is preferable to having the details of your secret life splashed all over the Internet by noon tomorrow." I shrugged. "Who knows, maybe you'll even be behind bars by Friday. People don't like child predators."

Lang's nostrils flared. "Fine," he spat out bitterly. "Let's get this over with."

The four of us circled the side of the brick house, clinging to the shadows as much as possible. When we reached our white van, Trinity climbed into the driver's seat.

Jack opened the back door, shoved Lang inside, and jumped in behind him.

My hand curled around the open doorframe. "Stick to the plan. Drive to Alexandria and back and don't go more than three miles over the speed limit."

With shaking hands, Trinity shoved the keys into the ignition. "Got it."

"And don't stop no matter what you hear."

She smirked and turned up the radio. "Don't worry about me. Now get back there so we can get this over with and get to bed."

"Yes, Jones. Did anyone ever tell you that you're bossy?"

She shoved me playfully in the chest. "Too many times to count."

By the time I joined Jack and Lang, Jack had

removed one of Lang's handcuffs and secured it around a metal bar on the far wall of the van. On the outside, it looked like a typical van used by a plumber or an HVAC company, but Jack and I had reconfigured the inside for interrogation and surveillance. A gray leather bench stretched along one side of the van, wrapping around the back, and computer equipment spanned the length of the other side. A metal partition separated the rear from the driver's compartment.

Settling into the open spot next to Jack, I leaned forward and flipped on a switch and pressed a few buttons to start recording our conversation. The administration and the justice department wanted this blackmail scheme to disappear without the public knowing about it. Officially, they claimed they didn't want to shake the public's belief in the integrity of Congress and the sanctity of members' votes during an election year. I didn't buy it. In my opinion, they wanted to bury this scandal because it crossed party lines. For them, it was a political class problem, not a party problem. Without fail, political insiders will bend over backward to defend the status quo by protecting those at the top and their agendas, which meant this problem had to disappear without a trace.

I slanted my body so I could see Lang's entire face. "Do you want to start?"

Lang pursed his lips and his eyes were stark. "You obviously summoned me for a reason. Why don't you start?"

"Okay." I drummed my fingers on my thigh. "We'll make this short and sweet. I think you'll do exactly as we tell you when you've heard everything."

Lang flicked his free hand, smiling dismissively. "Yes, so you said on the phone yesterday."

I nodded. "Approximately six months ago, you lobbied heavily against a bill expanding trade with Russia, citing concerns about systemic corruption and Russia's tendency to subsidize key industries to the detriment of U.S. exporters. At the last minute, you voted for the bill."

"I remember." He shrugged, the handcuffs clanking against the metal bar. "I talked to some of my colleagues and changed my mind. I'm not the first Representative to change my mind on a controversial issue. I won't be the last."

"Are you acquainted with Dima Antonov?" I asked. Antonov was a Russian businessman suspected of being involved in large-scale, cross-border tax fraud violations and market manipulations. He was on my short list of people who may have hired Miles to carry out the blackmail scheme.

"I've heard of him, but I've never met him."

I turned to Jack. "Can you pull up that photo we discussed?"

"Sure." Jack leaned forward and called up a photo of Miles and Lang on the monitor in front of me.

"Do you recall this meeting?"

Unbelievably, the bastard had the gall to smirk. "I'm pretty busy. I don't recall every conversation or meeting I have."

I flipped off the monitor and folded my arms

across my chest. "Fair enough. I'll cut the bullshit. When you were a high school gym teacher, you coerced more than one underage boy into a sexual relationship."

Lang's face turned beet red and his eyebrow twitched. "That's not true."

I cocked an eyebrow. "I have copies of the non-disclosure agreements you made the victims sign in exchange for a shit ton of money, and the corresponding wire transfers."

Lang leaned back and tipped his head to the ceiling. "You're bluffing."

I smirked. "Actually, I'm not. I lifted them off your computer at your fundraiser. Do you want me to pull up a copy?"

"So what?" His jaw flexed. "There is no admission in that agreement. They blackmailed me and in the interest of expediency, I settled."

"Wouldn't it be nice if that was the only evidence? Jack, go ahead and pull up those pictures."

Lang's eyes flared. "What pictures?"

Leaning forward, Jack's hands flew over a keyboard. "You should've seen my face when I stumbled onto these pictures. I didn't realize people could be this stupid. What kind of person keeps a photo record of their crimes?" Jack waved his hand. "That was a rhetorical question."

I scoffed. "No one ever claimed intelligence was a requirement for being elected to the House of Representatives."

Jack flipped through shadowy images of Representative Lang in various compromising positions with clearly underage boys. My stomach rolled, and I turned my attention to Lang instead of the monitor. After six clicks of the mouse, Jack minimized the images. "There's more, but I think we all understand what's happening in those pictures."

Lang closed his eyes and ran a hand over his face. "What do you want? Money? Favorable business deals? Insider information? I can send more government contracts your way."

I clenched my hands to stop myself from strangling him. He had ruined people's lives. He endangered our national security, and I didn't see a lick of remorse on his face. He belonged behind bars, but it wouldn't happen. Like too many before him, he was too big to fail.

"We want you to resign effective immediately."

His eyes popped open. "What?" He moved his head from side to side. "No. Absolutely not. I've worked hard to get where I am."

"You have forty-eight hours to announce your resignation due to health concerns or these pictures will be delivered to the appropriate law enforcement officers in your district, the media, and the FBI. You'll lose everything. Your freedom. Your reputation. Your fortune."

His gaze swiveled to meet mine. "What do you expect me to do for the rest of my life?"

My gut churned. I hated this. He should spend the rest of his life rotting in jail. Instead, he'd get away with a slap on the wrist if he agreed to my terms. "You're going to move back to your hometown and live a quiet life. If you even dip your pinkie toe into anything political, this offer will be retracted immediately, and I will expose you for the fraud you are."

His Adam's apple bobbed. "That's it? That's all you want?"

"Yes."

"If I do this, will you destroy those pictures and any other incriminating evidence?"

"No, but I can give you my word that no one will see them unless you break the agreement." He didn't answer for a second, and I thought he'd refuse. "I suggest you take this deal. A man like you won't fare very well in prison."

"Fine." He sighed as he rubbed a trembling hand down his face. "You have a deal."

CHAPTER TWENTY-NINE

Trinity

I cracked open my eyes and met Knox's soft stare. He dragged me closer to him, stopping only when my breasts smashed into his chest. Heat pooled deep in my belly and I slid my leg over the top of his, wanting to be closer to him.

"Good morning," I said, my voice rough from sleep.

"More like afternoon." His thumb stroked over my lips and my eyes fluttered, savoring his touch.

"Hmm," I said, hooking my arm around his shoulder, pulling him a few inches closer. "Well, we didn't get home until four in the morning so that makes sense."

With a half smile, he angled up my chin. "Thanks for helping last night." His lips moved against mine tenderly.

"Which part? Driving the van in circles in the

dead of the night or what happened when we got home?" I asked, already breathless.

He laughed, mischief dancing in his too-blue eyes. His warm fingers trailed up the outside of my thighs, setting off mini-explosions underneath my skin.

"Well, I was thanking you for driving us around, but I definitely enjoyed what happened later." He rolled on top of me, bracing his weight on his splayed hands, his muscles rippling. "But now that I think about it, my memory is a little fuzzy. Maybe we could reenact it, and I'll have something else to thank you for."

"Mm," I murmured as his lips brushed over mine. "I like that idea. I think I could use a refresher, too. I barely remember a thing after we got home." I lifted my arms over my head, stretching lazily. "In fact, what happened to my clothes?"

"I distinctly remember tearing them off five seconds after we made it through the door." His lips moved down my neck to my collarbone, and I felt the brush of stubble against my skin. "But I don't think you'll need them for a while."

I arched, my body already buzzing like I had champagne in my veins. "I'm okay with that if you make it worth my time."

He chuckled, the sound so deep and rich it curled my toes. "How generous of you."

His tongue swirled over my nipple, and I moaned. "Don't worry. You're on the right track."

"Good to know." I felt the corners of his lips curve up against my belly, and I couldn't stop the answering smile on my face. I wanted this morning to last forever. With his arms around me, and his mouth trailing down my feverish skin, I felt sheltered from everything and anything for the first time in forever. I knew I should care that I still had to talk to my brother. I knew the threat against my sister and me hadn't vanished. But it felt good to be distracted. Being with Knox obliterated all of the bad stuff because I wasn't alone. He was on my side. We were a team.

My stomach clenched under the swirling assault of his tongue as it dipped into my navel. "You're killing me," I whispered, mostly to myself.

He lifted his head. "Surrendering already?"

"No. Keep going."

A ringing noise floated through the air, dragging me unwillingly back to reality.

"Shit." He rested his forehead against my stomach. "I need to get that. It's Jack's ringtone. I told him to call me if there was any news about Lang. I'm sorry."

My stomach dipped with disappointment, but I pushed it back, ruffling my hands through his golden hair, enjoying the silken texture between my fingers. "It's okay."

"No. It's really not." He rolled off me, the bed squeaking as he snatched his phone from the nightstand. He twirled it in his hand for a beat. "Maybe I should turn it off for a few days. No interruptions. Just the two us. We could even take a trip away from here. How does that sound?"

I laughed, knowing he wasn't serious. "Just answer it. I'll make coffee and something to eat while you talk to Jack."

"As long as we continue where we left off after we eat." He swiped his finger along the screen of his phone.

"Sounds like a plan."

He turned around, sitting with his back to me, his bare feet planted on the floor. "Hello."

Giving him privacy, I kicked the sheets off, pulled on his discarded shirt, and padded down the hallway to the bathroom. I brushed my teeth and washed my face. I dug out some mascara and lip-gloss from my cosmetic case. I stared at my reflection in his brightly lit mirror. My lips were swollen. My hair was snarled. But my eyes glowed with happiness, and it hit me. I hadn't felt this happy or hopeful since the morning before my mom disappeared without a trace nearly fifteen years ago.

Uneasiness snaked around my chest, and for a second, I couldn't move. The mascara and lipstick slipped from my fingers, clattering onto the countertop and rolling to the tiled floor. I wasn't in love with Knox, right? This was just a hook-up between two people in the right place at the right time who enjoyed each other's company.

Images of the last few days and last night played through my mind. I bowed my head, gripping the edge of the countertop while my mind caught up with my heart. *Fuck!* If I wasn't already in love with Knox, I was tipping over the edge of sanity. I should reel my emotions in and concentrate on my life, so I wouldn't get hurt. I couldn't handle another failed relationship right now.

I needed to go back to my place and put it into some kind of order. Reality couldn't wait any longer. Neither could my talk with Derrick. He'd sidestepped all my requests to meet him, but I was going to put my foot down today. I refused to be ruled by another man's two-decade old sins any longer.

I twisted my hair up into a bun and made my way back to Knox's bedroom with every intention of putting some space between us for a few days.

"Hey." I froze mid-step, my brows pulling together. He was completely dressed.

He glanced over his shoulder as he slid his wallet into the back pocket of his jeans. "I need to head out, but you can stick around and help yourself to whatever you want."

"Oh, okay." My stomach dropped. I should've been happy I didn't need to come up with an excuse not to spend the day with him, but I wasn't. "Did something happen with Representative Lang?"

"Yeah." He pinched the bridge of his nose. "His housekeeper found him dead this morning."

"How?" I asked, feeling disoriented and more than a little dizzy.

"A self-inflicted gunshot wound to the head, or at least that's what it looks like."

My eyes widened as my whole body sagged. "Holy shit." I'd worked for Miles for over a year. Most of our missions centered on gathering information. I'd never been involved in anything where someone ended up dead; at least to the best of my knowledge.

He caught me around my wrist and gathered me close to him. The palms of his hands moved in smooth, even strokes up and down my arms. "Hey.

It's okay. I should have warned you this was a possibility."

"You knew he'd kill himself?" I sounded lost and vulnerable. I didn't even understand why I cared. I'd seen a few of those photos on his computer. Lang was a child predator. I knew that, but his death made everything seem more severe, more inescapable. The reality of it hit me with the force of a ton of bricks.

His hands framed my face. "I didn't know anything for certain. Are you upset?"

"No. Not really." I pushed away the uncomfortable feeling in my gut. "Just shocked."

"Are you going to be okay here by yourself?"

"Really. I'm fine." I swallowed, my throat feeling unbearably dry. "I'm actually going to head home today and clean up the mess. Maybe I can get Leslie to help me. It'd be nice to spend the afternoon with her."

I'd been living with Knox for over two weeks. Other than stopping by her bar before we had dinner, I hadn't made any effort to see her. I dodged her phone calls and ignored her texts because I didn't want to explain my actions or my relationship with Knox. She wouldn't approve, and I cared what she thought.

He nodded. "That's a good idea. I had someone clean up your place, but he left your clothes in a pile. I didn't know if you'd be comfortable with a stranger organizing your closet and drawers."

"Thanks." I lifted onto my tiptoes and pressed a kiss to his lips. My fingers curled around his neck, holding him like he was a lifeline. Like I was drowning, and he was the only thing keeping me above the surface. Even though I needed space to think, I didn't want to let him go.

He stepped back, eyeing me through the fall of his thick lashes, the smallest smirk on his face. "I need to get going, but I'll see you tonight. You're coming back here, right?"

I shifted my gaze to the floor, studying the chipped baby blue polish on my toes. "Yeah, I think so."

"Good." He reached around me, grabbing his keys off the dresser. "I don't think you should stay at your townhouse alone. Not until we figure out who's threatening you and your sister."

The minute Knox walked out, I fired off a text to Leslie asking her to stop by my place. By the time I arrived at my townhome, my thoughts were bouncing all over, and I felt like an emotional wreck.

"You beat me here," I said as I padded up my front steps.

"Hey." Leslie lifted her head, a huge smile on her face. "I'm glad you texted me. I was starting to think you were mad at me."

I jammed my key into the lock and pushed the door open with my hip. "Yeah. Sorry about that. I've been really busy."

She slung her tote bag over her shoulder and followed me inside. "I noticed. I stopped by two nights ago, but you didn't answer the door."

I paused in the entry. Knox's guys did a good job. My house smelled fresh. Everything was back in order. Even the sofa looked normal. They probably flipped the cushions to hide the damage.

I dropped my purse on the long console table and retrieved a bottle of wine and two glasses from the kitchen. "I've been staying with Knox."

"Wow." She blinked. "Things are moving fast between you two."

"It's not like that." I poured the wine into the glasses, then rubbed my hands together, deciding what to tell her. I settled on a half-truth. "Someone broke into my house, trashed everything, and my cat is gone." My voice shattered on the last word, and I silently prayed she wouldn't force me to go into the gory details. "I didn't want to stay here alone."

She frowned. "What the hell, Trinity? That's crazy." She paused, then her eyes widened. "Wait. What do you mean Max is gone? Gone as in missing or gone as in dead?"

I pressed the heels of my hands against my eyes for a second, fighting back tears. "He's dead, but I can't talk about that right now," I pleaded, my voice low and urgent. "Not yet. Okay?"

"All right." She nodded. "But I don't get it. Why didn't you call me? I would've let you stay with me."

"I tried, but Knox insisted I stay with him."

"Huh." She cocked her hip to the side. "And how's that going?"

"I don't know." I flopped onto the sofa. "Good. I think. I like him. I really like him, but I'm scared."

She sat next to me. "Scared of what?"

"Everything. My relationship with Miles was a mess, and I ignored all the signs."

She squeezed my hand. "Don't beat yourself up over Miles. Everybody needs a shitty ex or two so you know when you've found someone worth your time."

I tipped up my head and closed my eyes. "Maybe you're right. I'm just so confused."

"About Miles or Knox?"

My eyes popped open. "I don't give a shit about Miles. I don't know if I ever felt anything more than friendship for him, but Knox…"

She elbowed me. "Knox what?"

A smile tugged at the corner of my lips. "Even when I hate him, I like him. The last month has been the worst and the best month of my life. All this earth shattering stuff has happened, but when I'm with him, I feel sheltered and safe." I turned to face her. "I don't even know if that makes sense."

She laughed, a light tinkling noise that was so her. "Not at all."

I sat, staring at the wall, thinking over the last month. With Miles and every man before him, I pretended to be who I thought they wanted. Leslie said it was because I wanted them to accept me, but I didn't think she was right. In truth, I couldn't take facing the sting of rejection. I had a lifetime's worth of it bottled inside me from my mom's unexplained disappearance.

Yet I fell asleep night after night in Knox's arms, revealing tiny parts of myself piece-by-piece, even though I knew it was like flirting with a stick of dynamite. My uncle told me the ones I loved the most would hurt me the most, and I finally understood what he meant. I loved Knox. His rejection would crush me.

"I'm in love with Knox," I said quietly, fear

coiling around my chest. "I don't even understand it myself, but I am."

Leslie's eyes flared, confusion and concern etched into every line on her face. "Trinity, sweetheart, I don't know what to say."

I lifted one shoulder, then dropped it. "There's nothing to say. It's already done. I can't hit the rewind button and make it go away."

Groaning, she threw her hands into the air. "What about him? Does he love you?"

"I don't know." I sounded lost to my own ears.

She rolled her eyes. "What does your gut say?"

I kicked off my shoes and pulled my legs up to my chest. Being with Knox made me feel alive. Sometimes when he looked at me with barely concealed lust simmering in the depths of his clear blue eyes, my heart raced and my entire body tingled with excitement. I hoped he felt something similar for me. "That it's possible."

Her lips flattened and turned down at the corners. "This whole thing is crazy. I'm worried about you."

I smiled halfheartedly. "Don't be."

"Are you going to stay with him tonight?"

"I haven't decided." I rubbed the back of my neck as I dug my phone out of my pocket. "I was thinking I'd back away for a couple of days. I could use some space to sort through my feelings."

She nodded. "That's a good idea. Things went so fast with Miles. One day he was your boss and the next day you were together. Don't make the same mistake."

I stared at my phone, mulling over my options. Everything was so damn confusing. I had so many things to sort through. I didn't know where to start. I took a deep drink of my wine as if all of the answers could be found at the bottom of my glass. Sighing, I typed a quick message to Knox.

I have some stuff to take care of. I won't be back tonight. I'll be in touch soon.

My hand hovered over the phone for a moment before I pressed the *send* button. Leslie was right. I needed a breather. I needed to take a step back while I still could.

My conviction didn't last long. The minute Leslie left, guilt, regret, and loneliness overwhelmed me. I forcibly redirected my thoughts.

I thought about the all the things he'd done for me.

How I felt when I was with him.

How he smiled at me like I was special.

Somehow, I convinced myself he must really love me and he wouldn't walk away forever if I asked for space. I fell asleep on the sofa, clinging to that idea.

CHAPTER THIRTY

Knox

It was past ten o'clock in the evening when I jogged up Trinity's front steps and rang her doorbell. I had tried to sleep and give her the space she wanted, but I couldn't do it. I needed to see her in person.

Trinity opened her door and rubbed a hand down her face. Her dark hair was piled on her head. She wore a faded blue t-shirt that stopped at the top of her thighs.

"Why didn't you come back to my place tonight?"

Silence fell between us, thick and heavy.

She shifted uneasily. "I sent you a text. Didn't you get it?"

"I did, but it wasn't much of an explanation." I peered over her shoulder, my hand resting on the doorframe. "Can I come in?"

Staring at the floor, she scraped her teeth over her lower lip. "Sure." She opened the door wider, and I stepped inside. She didn't say anything, so I filled the space with meaningless words. "The place looks good."

She blew out a ragged breath. "Knox, why did you come here tonight?"

This woman had me on edge. Somehow or another, without even trying, she'd managed to climb inside my head and screw up all my plans. I'd been content with my life until she'd stormed into Lang's study with her gun pointed at me. I never imagined I would get so wrapped up in a woman that I would want her at my side and in my life as much as I did with Trinity.

It happened too fast, almost like a train wreck. I had this preconceived notion that when I hit my mid-thirties, I'd get bored with the status quo and slowly but surely move to the next step in life—a more permanent girlfriend or even a wife. But this heady, nerve-wracking, merry-go-round with Trinity was insane. And here was the biggest mind fuck of all—if I were honest with myself, I'd have to admit the feelings I had for Trinity sure as hell resembled love, and I never planned on love.

My mom fell in and out of love as fast as the wind shifted. She always thought the next love affair would be her salvation, but every last one of those men used her. And she let it happen. She served herself up on a silver platter over and over again. As crude as it sounded, she was a high paid escort with a *Pretty Woman* fantasy. Love ruined people, or at least I thought so, but now something told me I had it all wrong. Maybe love wasn't about ruin or salvation. Maybe it was about living your life with the one person who made it bigger, brighter and more worthwhile.

I rubbed the back of my neck. "I missed you tonight. I couldn't sleep."

She shuffled her bare feet. "I…I don't know what to say."

"Just say what's going on in your head. Tell me why you changed your mind about staying with me tonight," I said calmly.

She tugged on the hem of her shirt. "I don't know where to start."

I shoved my hands into my pockets. "Start with the truth."

"I just needed a break from us." She rolled her shoulders back. "I'm confused and I wanted some alone time."

My muscles tensed, and I balled my hands into fists, my gut sinking. Maybe I misunderstood everything, and I'd been wrong to think the past few days had been anything more than a fleeting affair. "About what?"

Sighing, she took a couple steps back. "I just ended things with Miles. My life as I know it is dangling from a thread. I'm worried about Derrick and my sister. I don't know. I'm pretty much a mess."

Hurt twisted inside my gut. "Is this your way of ending things between us?"

"It's just one night." She rolled her head in a circle. "Maybe two."

I cocked an eyebrow. "Is it?"

"I don't know, Knox." She wrung her hands in front of her chest. "I just feel like this is going too fast, and I wanted to take a step back."

A large part of me wanted her to give us a stay of execution and draw this out for another night. But every second I spent with her would only make it tougher to walk away later.

"I'm an adult, Trinity. We both are. You don't have to dance around your feelings in order to spare mine. Just say what you want instead of dragging this out."

"I like you. A lot. I don't know what I would've done without you for the past few weeks. You've supported me, you put my home back together, and you've given me a place to stay. So many things." She swallowed. "But we need to go back to the real world. You've got your company to run, you have to finish your case and all the stuff that goes along with that."

"Wow." My eyebrows shot up my forehead. "So that's it? You're done with us?"

She trained her gaze on the floor. "I think it's probably for the best. At least temporarily, anyway."

I tipped up her chin, forcing her to look at me. "For who? You? Me? Miles? Or your brother?"

She shook her head. "I'm not saying this is it forever. It's just no for right now. I need to get this sorted out with Derrick, and I don't want to drag you through the inevitable minefield with me."

I ran my fingertips down her arm. "I don't care about that. You need someone to support you. Let me be there for you, even if it's only as a friend. I'm not giving up on us."

"Thank you for the offer." She smiled gently.

"But this is something I need to do alone, and I always have Leslie."

"Have you heard from Derrick?"

She kept her face carefully blank. "No."

"Will you call me when you meet with him? I want to go with you." Trinity might feel comfortable with him, but I didn't trust him.

"Knox." She drew out my name. "I can't bring you with me. You're investigating him and even though he may have done something wrong, I won't facilitate his downfall. He may not have been part of my life for long, but he's still my half-brother, and I need all the family I can get. I don't want him to alienate me forever because I destroyed his life."

Anger surged through my veins, but I tamped it down as fast as it came. Yelling at her wouldn't help. It'd only push her further away, and I sure as hell didn't want to force any more distance between us.

"So you're going to play by his rules and keep his secret as long as he wants."

"I can't answer that question right now. I haven't decided what the end game is. Our lives are tied together—"

"Dammit, Trinity." I clenched my jaw, barely holding my temper in check. "This isn't just about keeping the Benton family skeletons in the closet. He's the Speaker of the House, and he's allowing a foreign government to sway his decisions. His votes. Everything, so he can spare his family the embarrassment of a two-decade-old scandal. Wake up. He's endangering national security. Don't you get it? There's no going back anymore. Just like

Lang, he's going to lose everything. It's only a matter of time. Once I have enough evidence, he will resign."

Her eyes widened. "What kind of evidence are you looking for?"

I shrugged. "Anything that definitely demonstrates he's changed his votes or actions under the threat of blackmail. It could be as simple as the testimony of someone with insider knowledge."

Her face whitened, and it hit me. She knew. He told her everything. She'd been holding back. "Trinity, did he confess to you?"

"Stop. I can't talk about it." She covered her face, shaking her head. "I'll get him to come clean, so neither of us has to worry about someone holding it over our heads in the future. I can't deal with the rest right now."

Stunned, I propped my elbow on the fireplace mantle, my head leaning against my hand. "You have to tell me what you know."

She pressed her open palm against my chest, her eyes wide and pleading. "Please, Knox, give me a couple of days to get Derrick to do the right thing before you make me turn on him."

"Fucking hell." My hand pummeled the wall. The picture of Trinity and her sister clattered to the floor, tiny glass shards showering the slab marble hearth. "Why did you lie to me?"

A tortured groan escaped her parted lips. "I didn't lie. Not really. I just didn't tell you."

Anger wrapped around me and my chest tightened. "An omission and a lie are the same fucking thing."

Tears leaked out of the corners of her eyes and a strangled sob tumbled from her lips. "I'm sorry. I wanted to exhaust all our alternatives before I told you. I know it was wrong, maybe even a little delusional, but I thought I could find a loophole that would make everyone happy."

My teeth locked together. I needed to get out of here. I couldn't look at her. I fucking loved this woman. I told her some of my darkest secrets. I invited her into my life, and she didn't even trust me. I stalked to the front door without looking at her.

"You have forty-eight hours."

She grabbed my hand, her eyes wild. "Don't hate me. Don't push me away."

I scoffed, bitter, cutting laughter flowing from my mouth. "You're the one doing the pushing, not me, darling." My voice was hard and mocking, but I couldn't stop myself. Her lack of trust made me feel like she'd hollowed out my chest with a spoon.

"Oh my God." She tugged on the front of my shirt. "Please tell me I didn't ruin us."

I threw my hands into the air. "Why do you care? You already told me you needed space. There is no us."

"I'm sorry. I'm so fucking sorry." She draped her arms around my shoulders, bringing her body flush against mine. It felt right to have her in my arms, which only pissed me off more. "This is killing me. You're the only thing that's kept me sane in the past month. I wish this would all go away, and I could concentrate on you because I'm falling so hard for you. You know that, right?" She tipped up her head, her dark gaze meeting mine. "But wishing and hoping won't change reality. I need to work things out with Derrick and figure out a solution I can live with."

Tired of all the games, secrets, and lies, I pried her arms off my neck. "Like I said, you have forty-eight hours. That's all I can give you. After that, you're on your own. I can't wait any longer. I have a job to do."

"Thank you. I'll make it work." She brushed her hand down the side of my face. "When this is behind us, do you think you can find it in your heart to give me a second chance?" I opened my mouth to respond, and she pressed a finger to my lips. "You don't have to answer now. I just wanted to put it out there so you know how I feel. My decision to put space between us has nothing to do with how I feel about you."

Uncertainty billowed between us. She fisted her hands in my shirt, her chocolate eyes rife with confusion and insecurity. I'd never seen such depth in a pair of eyes. I wanted to pull her into my arms, but I didn't. I stepped back, breaking her hold. As my hand curled around the door handle, a million sentiments swirled on the tip of my tongue, begging for freedom.

I wanted to tell her I loved her.

That I'd wait for her.

That I needed her in my life.

I didn't say any of those things. Instead, the anger won out, and I drove a stake into both our hearts. "Don't worry about us. You made the right choice. Just don't do anything stupid. We still don't know who's behind the notes." My words were subdued, sullen. I shook my head, hating myself for acting like a pussy and hating her for being able to walk away from me so easily.

A weighted sigh escaped her lips. "Thanks for everything, Knox Black."

CHAPTER THIRTY-ONE

Trinity

"Uncle Mac?" I smiled faintly, tilting my head to the side, and he frowned. "What are you doing here?"

My uncle glanced over his shoulder and popped up the collar of his worn black leather jacket. He looked exactly as I remembered except he had a few more wrinkles around his eyes and his beard was more gray than strawberry blond these days.

His eyes narrowed. "You look like shit."

I folded my arms across my chest. "Well, thanks. So do you."

He didn't say anything my reflection hadn't told me when I looked in the mirror this morning. My eyes were puffy from crying myself to sleep. I hadn't bothered with makeup, and I'd barely run a brush through my hair, but he didn't need to point it out. Not that his comment shocked me. He'd always been blunt and to the point.

"That's no way to talk to your uncle. I haven't seen you in over three years. Why don't you invite me inside?"

I twisted my leather bracelet around my wrist, not answering him for a second. After Knox had left last night, I sent dozens of texts to Derrick, begging him to meet me today. After thirty minutes of back and forth messaging, I threatened to reveal our connection with or without his support. He finally responded this morning with a brisk text instructing me to come to his house at one o'clock sharp.

"I was just about to leave. I have an appointment soon."

"This won't take long. I need to tell you a few things about your mother."

My heart skipped inside my chest. "Hold on. Let me get my purse and we can grab a coffee."

"You're wasting your money on that shit."

I rolled my eyes. "My coffee machine is broken."

The carafe had been one of the victims of the ransacking of my apartment. Instead of running out for coffee, I'd spent the morning composing and deleting texts to Knox. In the end, I turned off my phone without sending anything. What could I say? Nothing had changed since last night.

"So tell me about Mom," I said, as we walked down the front steps of my townhome.

"First, I want you to tell me why you look like you spent last night crying."

I huffed. "I had a fight with some guy I'm seeing. I don't want to talk about it."

He hooked one arm around my shoulder. He still smelled like leather and cigarette smoke. "You'll figure it out, and if he's stupid enough to walk away from you, then good riddance." His eyes swept over my face. "You're even more beautiful than your mother. Did I ever tell you that?"

I chuckled weakly. "I don't think you ever told me much of anything about my mom. You preferred to pretend like she didn't exist," I said, purposely changing the subject because I didn't want to think about how my cowardice may have spoiled any chance I had with Knox. Just thinking about him, what I did, and what we could've had made me the kind of miserable that ate at my gut like I had swallowed a gallon of acid. When I woke up this morning, sadness wrapped around my body like a shroud. I couldn't stop replaying the look on his face when I asked for space.

"Yeah. You're right." His arm slipped from my shoulder and he smiled, but it didn't reach his eyes.

I yanked open the door to the coffee shop at the end of my block. The coffee they served tasted more burnt than anything else, but my caffeine-fueled withdrawal had resulted in a dull ache inside my head, so I couldn't be picky. "How's Faith?"

He shrugged, his leather jacket creaking. "About the same. She doesn't come around much, but you probably already know that."

I ordered a large black coffee and stuffed the change into the tip jar. "I don't hear from her much either, except an occasional text about tuition."

"Yeah." He nodded, his lips spreading into a thin line. "I didn't think so. She was pretty pissed when you moved to D.C."

We settled into a booth at the back of the coffee shop. I stared at him over the rim of my paper cup. "Are you going to talk about my mom or did you change your mind?"

He leaned forward, sliding his elbows over the table. "I should have told you this before you moved to D.C., but I didn't want to worry you." He blew out a breath. "The day your mom disappeared, she planned to meet up with someone who represented your biological father. She said he agreed to a financial settlement in exchange for her silence. She was over the moon." He shook his head, his gaze drifting to the side. "She had all these plans for you and Faith. She wanted to buy a house and put down some roots instead of floating around."

I curled my hands around the edge of the table. "So what happened?"

"I don't know for sure."

I twisted the coffee cup sleeve. "What do you think happened?"

He scrubbed his hand down the side of his beard. "I think Richard Benton had her killed."

My hand jerked and my coffee tipped over. Brown liquid spread across the table. My hands shaking, I tossed a stack of napkins on the table, blotting up the mess. "That doesn't make any sense," I whispered, my gaze fluttering from table to table looking for anyone eavesdropping on our conversation.

"I don't know for sure, but I got a letter a few days after she disappeared." He shifted in his seat. "I can't remember the exact wording, but it basically told me to shut up, or we'd all end up dead."

My heart skidded to a halt, and I shuddered. "Why didn't you go to the police?"

"Because I'm an ex-con, and the last thing I needed was the police sniffing around me. I'd come a long way since my ass landed in prison, but I hadn't exactly kept my nose clean. They would've taken you and Faith away and stuck you in foster care." He balled up the coffee drenched napkins. "I wasn't the best role model, but your mom and I spent the last five years of our childhood in foster care. I wouldn't wish it on my worst enemy."

I drew in a fractured breath as I nodded absently. I knew what he was talking about. My mom told me a few things about foster care. Most people would consider my uncle a below average guardian, but he didn't abuse us. We had clothes. We had food. We had a roof over our head, but we didn't have an outpouring of love or emotional support. He was essentially a roommate who paid the bills.

"Are you sure the letter was about my mom and not some of the things you did in your past?"

He scratched the side of his neck. "Yeah," he admitted. "I won't lie. There's some ugly stuff in my past. Stuff that would make people nervous. Stuff that might be worth killing or threatening me over, but the people in my past don't hide behind letters. They deliver their messages in person accompanied by a good ass-kicking."

A chill zipped down my spine. "Why now? Why didn't you tell me years ago?"

"Because people have been asking questions

about you over the last six months."

My brows scrunched together. "Asking who?"

He shrugged and rolled his thick neck in a circle. "Your old friends and acquaintances. The questions seemed kind of innocuous in the beginning. They wanted to know if you ever talked about your parents. Then they started throwing around your biological father's name and asked if you ever talked about him or mentioned him by name." He leaned forward. "Have you been in contact with them? Did you move here to be closer to them?"

"Who?" I drew circles on my jeans, avoiding his eyes, pretending I didn't understand his question.

"The Bentons," he hissed. "Don't play dumb with me, girl. I've known you too long for that."

My head snapped up. "I moved here because my half-brother asked me to. He said he wanted to get to know me. He helped me find a place to live, and we're friendly."

Leaning back, he folded his arms across his chest, a pained sound scraping out of his mouth. "Jesus, Trinity. What the hell are you thinking? The Bentons will destroy you. You're a stain on their reputation. It's only a matter of time before they grind you into the dirt."

"You're wrong. Derrick cares about me. He wouldn't hurt me." My words broke. My heart splintered. My chest ached. I didn't want to believe him. I couldn't. It hurt too much. I pushed Knox away, at least temporarily, to support Derrick. It'd gut me if I did it for nothing. "He found me because he wanted me to be in his life."

His fist collided with the top of the table and my

empty cup tipped over again. "You're a fool if you believe that. He contacted you because the Bentons have an agenda. I want you to pack up your shit and come home with me today."

"No." I jumped out of my seat, gathering my purse and the coffee-soaked paper napkins as fast as possible. I refused to fall apart in front of my uncle. "I'm not running away from this."

He shook his head. "What are you going to do? Stick around and wait for them to kill you, too?"

"I don't know. I'll call you later. I need to process everything you told me." With my head down and my hands shoved deep into my pockets, I half-ran, half-walked out the door.

CHAPTER THIRTY-TWO

Knox

"Do you want to talk about it?" Jack said.

Ignoring Jack, my fingers flew over the keyboard as I typed an email to Archer. Last night, after two hours of searching for clues as to how I misjudged Trinity's feelings for me, I didn't come up with anything. Instead of wallowing in self-pity, I decided to do something productive. I spent the entire night uploading security updates to Black Investments' server.

"Hello." Jack waved his hand in front of my face. "Talk to me."

"There's nothing to talk about," I answered without looking at him.

Jack shoved his chair away from the table, the wheels rumbling across the floor. "What the hell happened in the last twenty-four hours? Yesterday you walked around with this stupid 'I'm in love' smile, and today you look like you want to kick someone's ass."

I closed my laptop. "I didn't know you wanted to spend the day sharing feelings. Where should we start?" I propped my hands behind my head, glaring at him. "With your fucked up marriage or my non-existent relationship with Trinity?"

Jack chuckled. "Oh, so this is about Trinity Jones. Did she already dump your ass?" He shook his head. "Don't say I didn't warn you. I knew she was bad news."

Anger rushed through my veins. I stood, flexing my hands hard enough to make the tendons stand out. "You don't know anything, Jack, and unless you want me to crawl up your ass and start asking questions about your wife, you need to back the hell off."

"Fine." He held up his hands in mock surrender. "I'll back off, but I reserve the right to say 'I told you so' when the time comes."

My brows snapped together. "What do you mean?"

He rubbed his hand down his face. "Nothing. If you think you have everything under control, then I trust you."

An alert on my phone buzzed, and Jack, being closer to it, slid it across the table. "Speaking of Trinity, it looks like your girl is on the move again."

I picked up the phone and turned it in circles in one hand. "I don't know what you're talking about."

Smirking, he shook his head. "Right. Don't lie to me. In between ignoring me and pounding on your keyboard, you've been tracking her movements on your phone." He cleared his throat. "I'd never thought I'd live to see the day when Knox Black had his panties in a bunch over some chick."

"It's not like that. I'm worried about her." I swiped a finger across the phone, scanning the dot on the screen as Trinity moved across town.

"She's a big girl. She'll be just fine."

"Fuck!" I yelled, when I realized her destination.

Jack frowned. "What's going on?"

I stuffed my phone in my pocket and slung my jacket over my shoulder. "Trinity is headed to Miles Knightly's house."

Jack jumped out of his chair. "Do you think she's been spying on us for him?"

I stalked across the office and flung open the door. "I don't think so. She hates him, but she might get a hair up her ass and decide to confront him."

"Do you want me to go with you?"

"No." I shook my head. "I don't want to cause a scene."

"Are you sure?"

"Yeah. I'll call you if I need back-up."

CHAPTER THIRTY-THREE

Trinity

After a quick stop at my house and thirty minutes of wandering around D.C. on foot, I found myself in front of Miles's house. I pounded on his door. A gust of cool air whipped around my body and chills roughened my skin. Thick strands of my hair lashed the side my face and the silky material of my shirt billowed like a sail in the wind.

I should've called Knox and shared my plans, but I always hated being controlled and led around by the nose. Knox told me not to do anything stupid and this certainly qualified as stupid. Miles and I spent a lot of time together, but I really didn't know anything about him. Sure, I knew what he liked to order from his favorite Chinese restaurant. I knew he liked bourbon. I knew he had a daughter and an ex-wife who would never let him go, but those were just meaningless facts I could've discovered during a five-minute conversation.

Apprehension trickled down my spine, but I ignored it. Nothing bad would happen. I could take care of myself. Steeling my nerves, I squared my shoulders, and pounded on the door again.

"Trinity," Miles said wearily. "To what do I owe this pleasure?"

"How did you find out Speaker Benton is my half-brother?" I could've approached the subject with more eloquence, but I didn't have the time.

"I don't know anything about that." He peered over my shoulder, then started to push the door closed. "You shouldn't be here. You need to leave."

I smacked my hand into the door and pulled a gun out of the holster hidden inside my jacket, pushing my way into the house and shutting the door behind me. Knox had confiscated my gun of choice at Lang's house, but I also had a Kahr P380 hidden under a floorboard in my closet. Roughly the size of a cell phone, it was very concealable, but just as reliable and effective as larger models.

"I'm not going anywhere until I know the truth. I'm fucking sick of all the lies. Tell me how you found out about Derrick and me."

He held up his hands and backpedaled a few steps. "You're a lunatic. If you don't get out of here, I'll call the police."

"Be my guest." I jammed the barrel of my gun against his chest. "I'd be happy to talk to them about all your blackmail schemes. I'm sure there's plenty of evidence right here in your home. I'll even invite Knox over, and he can bring Lang's taped confession. He implicated you." He didn't, but

Miles had no way of knowing that.

Sasha, his ex-wife, glided into the room, her black maxi dress dusting the floor with every step. "Just tell the truth, Miles. This is getting old."

"Get the fuck out of here, Sasha. This is none of your business," Miles yelled through his teeth.

"No. I'm not listening to you. Not this time." She folded her arms across her chest. "You think you can spin some magic and end up with her share of the money, but it's not going to happen unless you put a gun to her head and force her down the aisle. And from where I'm standing, it looks like she's the one with the gun."

"The money?" My stare boomeranged between Miles and Sasha, helplessness seeping into my words. "What money?"

She rolled her eyes. "God, you're naïve. I don't know how Miles could stand being around you. You're like this hear no evil, see no evil chick, charging into things with her eyes closed, believing everyone has altruistic motives."

Miles pushed my gun away and pointed his finger at Sasha. "Shut up. This isn't a game."

"No, you shut up, Miles." I stared over their heads, unable to look at either one of them. "I want to hear what she has to say."

"Gladly." She flipped her long hair over her shoulder. "Didn't you wonder why Miles asked you to be his assistant, a woman with no college education whose only job experience was slinging drinks in a nightclub?"

My gaze cut to Miles, ice worming its way through my veins. "You came into Leslie's bar for weeks. We became friends.”

She snorted. “Yeah, sweetie, life doesn’t work that way. He went to that bar looking for you. He recruited you.”

Miles rested his chin against his chest. “Go away, Sasha. I need to talk to Trinity alone.”

She speared me with her eyes, her lips curling in disgust. “Fine, but if he doesn’t tell you the truth, I will. Keep that in mind.”

I didn’t respond.

Sasha disappeared down the hall, and the door to Miles’s study clicked shut.

“Go ahead,” I said, my voice thin and frail, my gun burning a hole in my hand.

He shifted on his feet. “Through one of my contacts, I learned the Benton family was hiding the details of Richard Benton’s illegitimate child.”

I met his gaze, chin lifted. “In the course of your blackmail scheme.”

His lips pressed together. “I’m not going to comment on that.”

“Fine.” I waved my hand, struggling to keep my voice as calm as possible. “Continue.”

“I found out your name and that Derrick Benton helped you relocate to D.C. at Richard Benton’s request.”

I frowned. “That doesn’t explain why you sought me out.”

He nodded slowly and stuffed his hands in his pockets. “All of Richard Benton’s money was put into a trust. His trust provided his wife with a generous monthly payment, along with the use of all his properties until her death. The remaining assets, however, were to be split equally between his children."

I sucked in a giant mouthful of air. "He only has one child. He never claimed me. His name isn't on my birth certificate."

"Well, none of that matters, because you're mentioned by name in his trust." When I didn't respond, he continued talking. "There's one caveat, however. You have to come forward and claim the money before your twenty-fifth birthday, otherwise your share reverts to Derrick, which is in—"

"Two months," I said, interrupting him.

He cleared his throat. "Yeah. Two months."

My eyes pinched closed for a split second. "So you planned to help me claim my share?"

He cringed. "Kind of."

Hate and bitterness churned in my gut like a gasoline fed bonfire. "That's why you wanted to get married. You were with me for the money. Money I didn't even know I had." My chin quivered, and I could feel the tears sneaking out of the corners of my eyes.

He held out his hand, but I slapped it away. "At first, but things changed. I cared about you. I still do."

"You're pathetic. Get away." The words scraped like glass across my lips. My vision blurred with a toxic combination of confusion and betrayal. I stood there, my feet rooted to the ground, trying to wrap my head around what he said. I didn't know how to absorb his confession. Grief crawled up the walls of my throat, warring for freedom.

Freedom to scream.

Freedom to rage.

Freedom to hurt someone else.

All of those emotions huddled inside of me like a ticking bomb. Slowly building. Enclosing my throat. Blinding me. I felt like I was breaking into a thousand jagged pieces.

Thud.

Thud.

Thud.

The doorknob rattled behind me.

"Open the door, Miles. I know Trinity's here."

My head shot up. "It's Knox," I whispered, whirling around to face the door. My mind unraveled, confusing emotions swirling like a tornado inside of me, and suddenly I knew he was the only thing in my life that made sense. I loved him. I needed him.

CHAPTER THIRTY-FOUR

Knox

Trinity opened the door. Tears spilled down her cheeks. A small handgun dangled from her fingers. Her shoulders sagged. She looked defeated.

"Knox." She dragged out my name, her voice low and reverent.

"Trinity." I scanned her for injuries, but other than her tears and puffy eyes, I didn't see anything. "What's going on? Why did you come here? You can't trust Miles."

Her gaze flicked to his, and she swallowed. "He used me. Derrick used me. It was all about the money."

"What money?"

With unsteady fingers, she stuffed the gun into her purse. "My half of the Benton Family Trust. Miles wanted to marry me for it. Derrick wanted to keep all of it."

I charged forward. Before I could stop myself, my hands circled Miles's neck and I shoved him into the wall. "What the hell is she talking about?"

"Ask her. She knows everything." His fingers clawed at my hands. "Get out of my house."

Trinity's hands hooked around the back my belt. "Let's go. I need to get out of here." I tightened my hold on Miles. "Please," she whimpered.

I glanced over my shoulder. Her entire body shook. Her eyes were wide and pleading. "Fine." My hands dropped from his neck, and I guided her out of the door, not bothering to shut it behind me.

She stood on the street, her head hanging down and her eyes pinched shut. "How did you find me?"

I stared down the street, trying to find a way to sugarcoat my answer. Nothing came to me, and I didn't want to lie to her anyway. We had both been subjected to enough lies. "I installed a tracking device on your phone after you agreed to work for me. I needed to know if you were being honest with me." I blew out a breath. "When I saw you go to Miles's house, I followed, not because I don't trust you, but because I don't trust him."

She rubbed her eyes. "I should be mad at you for so many reasons right now, but I'm glad you showed up. I wanted to kill Miles and his dumb ex-wife." She shook her head, her lips flat and her eyes dull. "I don't know what to do. I'm so lost right now."

Without a word, I edged up behind her and looped my arms around her waist. Her muscles tensed before she wilted into my embrace. I bent my head, my lips sliding along the slope of her neck and back up to her chin.

"We'll figure it out."

She tipped up her head, her dark eyes sizing me up, peering into my soul. "Did you know Richard Benton named me as a beneficiary of the Benton Family Trust? Did you know I have to make some claim on it before I turn twenty-five, which is in two months?"

"No." I rested my chin on top of her head. "But now it makes more sense why the Benton family wanted you to keep the connection secret."

She spun in my arms. "I'm sorry about last night. Don't hate me."

I glanced down at her, my throat tightening. "You're forgiven. Besides, I could never hate you." Now wasn't the time to throw mud at each other.

She made a harsh sound in the back of her throat, her face filling with dread and regret. "No. You should be mad. I put Derrick before you just because he's my brother, but he never earned it. Other than giving me some money and sparing a few hours of his time on occasion, he didn't earn my loyalty. You did."

I smiled crookedly. "I'll forgive you if you conveniently forget I was tracking your phone." I pressed my key fob.

"Hm. I'll think about it."

I opened the passenger door of my car. "Get in."

"Where are we going?" she asked as I pulled away from the curb.

"Back to your place."

She leaned forward, rubbing her hands together in front of the heat vent. "I was supposed to meet

Derrick at his house an hour ago."

"Cancel it."

Her pupils flared. "Why? I need to confront him more than ever. According to Miles, he wanted to keep my identity secret because he didn't want me to claim my share of the trust." She slumped in her seat, her chin resting against her chest.

"You're not meeting with him alone. We're hiring an attorney to get to the bottom of this. You can't trust anything Derrick says. Archer has people on retainer. They'll need to do a conflicts check, but we can probably get them to set up something as early as tomorrow."

"I don't think so." A bitter laugh spilled from my mouth. "Derrick will drag his feet as long as possible. He'll take this right down to the wire."

"No. He won't because we'll take your story straight to the media and he knows it. The only thing worse than revealing his father had an illegitimate daughter would be that he tried to screw you out of your inheritance."

She closed her eyes and leaned her shoulder against mine. "You know what's crazy? I don't even think I want the money. He could have convinced me to give it up. I just wanted to have him in my life. Maybe I should tell him he can keep the money."

"No," I said, my voice echoing inside the car.

Her eyelids unsealed, and she stared at me, bewildered. "Why not?"

"You shouldn't give up anything until you know everything. Maybe your dad left a message for you. Once you understand your rights and what the intent of the trust was, then you can do whatever you want, but don't make a half-cocked decision."

"Yeah, that makes sense." She sucked her lips into her mouth, and her voice dropped. "Can I ask you something?"

"Sure."

She turned her legs toward me. "Do you remember the night when you found me looking through your files?" Her voiced trailed off, and she picked at a loose thread on the hem of her shirt.

"Yes. I think you tried to steal a couple of them."

A wobbly smile spread across her face. "Well, I found a file with my mom's name on it. I didn't get a chance to look at it. Why were you researching her?"

My grip on the steering wheel tightened. "What is your mom's name again?"

"Anna Jones."

I wiped my hand across my lips, hesitating for a beat. "I didn't realize she was your mom."

"No." She glanced out the window. "Probably not. The name is pretty generic. Can I look at the file?"

"Sure." I pulled into the parking spot across the street from her townhome. "There's not much to see. I did a pretty basic background check on her. Nothing too invasive. Apparently, she worked in the Benton household for six months when she was eighteen. They terminated her employment and paid her twenty thousand dollars. I couldn't find much else about her after that." I squeezed her hand. "I thought she might know what Miles was using to blackmail Derrick Benton."

"I guess you were right." Her fingers closed around the door handle. "Did you ever find any traces of her?"

"She hasn't used her social security number in over a decade. She's never popped up on social media." I rubbed my hand down the side of my face. "Honestly, I didn't spend much time researching her because I concluded she was dead within minutes of scanning her background check. It seemed like a waste of time and resources."

She blanched, and a lungful of air wheezed between her lips. Tears brimmed in her eyes, overflowing down her cheeks. "My uncle thinks she's dead, too." She swallowed as if she was searching for courage. "He came to visit me this morning. That's why I went to Miles's house. I thought I could get him to tell me everything."

I reached across the console and pulled her into my arms. "It sounds like you did, but you shouldn't have confronted him alone."

Her chest heaved. "Not really. He told me about the trust and my brother, but I didn't get anything to help you find out who hired Miles."

"Shh." I smoothed my hand up and down the back of her hair. "One thing at a time. First, we'll deal with your brother. Then we can worry about Miles."

CHAPTER THIRTY-FIVE

Darcey Benton

I sat in a small artsy wine bar with exposed brick walls, round heating ducts spanning the length of the ceiling and wooden tables without tablecloths. I wore a black, blunt cut wig and a long black jacket with the collar popped. Luckily, I was able to secure a seat next to the window, which gave me a prime view of Trinity Jones's townhome.

Apparently, on Wednesday nights, the bar hosted aspiring musicians. A steady flow of melodramatic idiots with less than mediocre voices stood on a small stage, singing about hurt feelings, broken hearts and a bunch of other nonsense. The sheer silliness of it almost prompted me to abandon my plan, but I didn't have a choice.

Tomorrow would be too late. Derrick had caved to that opportunistic bitch's plans. So instead, I concentrated on the clogged traffic on the street and the river of people pouring in and out of the front door.

I should've eliminated my husband's bastard child long ago. Forcing Trinity's mother out of the house with a twenty thousand dollar check without making her take a pregnancy test was the biggest miscalculation I'd ever made. At the time, I thought I'd got off cheap. I would've paid ten times that amount to make my husband's child mistress disappear.

By the time I found out about the pregnancy, it was too late. For nearly ten years, Anna Jones drifted around the country, never staying anywhere for more than six months at a time. Finally, she settled down in that godforsaken town in Texas, and I lured her to her death with the promise of a huge monetary settlement in exchange for signing a non-disclosure agreement. I thought killing Anna Jones would be the end of the story.

Instead, my piece of shit husband suddenly found God when he became sick, and begged his son to find Trinity and bring her into the fold. My spineless son did exactly that. Fortunately, my husband's health deteriorated quickly, and I succeeded in persuading Derrick to keep the details of the trust private. He appeased his guilt by tossing money in Trinity's direction on occasion and renting a townhome owned by a Benton subsidiary to her at a reduced rate. Until recently, I was satisfied knowing that the money-grubbing whore's daughter would never get access to the Benton Family Trust.

I had earned every penny of that money with

blood, sweat, and tears. I overlooked my husband's repeated indiscretions, ill-treatment, and forty years of all around hell. I'd never willingly hand over half of the Benton family fortune to some no name bastard without an ounce of class or breeding. That money belonged to my son and my grandkids. Everything would've been perfect if Trinity Jones heeded my warnings, and kept her mouth closed, but she hadn't.

So I waited, watching for the lights to turn off inside Trinity's townhome. By the end of the night, I'd finally be rid of her once and for all. I'd kill her just like I did her mother. I couldn't hire someone else to do my dirty work. It was too big of a risk.

Derrick would go into a rage when he found I'd killed Trinity. He was a sentimentalist, and for some unknown reason, he had a soft spot for Trinity. This time tomorrow, Derrick would be having a tantrum rivaling that of a spoiled child, but I didn't care. I was doing this for him. Sooner or later, he'd understand that.

At ten o'clock in the evening, the lights in Trinity's townhome dimmed. I lingered for another two hours, ordering enough drinks not to raise any flags or trigger anyone's memory. For the tenth time that night, I checked the syringe in my pocket loaded with potassium chloride. Within minutes of injecting her, Trinity's heart would beat out of control and then stop functioning altogether. The coroner would rule sudden cardiac arrest as the cause of her death. And the nightmare that started over twenty-five years ago would finally be over.

With my head down, I slipped out of the

restaurant, darted across the street, and pulled the spare key to Trinity's home from my coat pocket.

CHAPTER THIRTY-SIX

Trinity

My head pounded from crying and not just in one area. It was the whole damn thing from the top of my head to the bottom of my jaw. Even my scalp hurt. I rolled onto my side, but that only increased the dull throbbing in my head. It was official. This had been one of the worst days of my life.

My emotions were all over the place. This morning I'd hopped out of bed determined to find the truth, then by mid-afternoon everything had exploded. The truth didn't seem so valuable any longer. I didn't know what I would've done without Knox. He hired an attorney to represent me who somehow finagled a meeting with Derrick and his attorney tomorrow evening. Then he carried me to bed and held me for hours while I'd wept over my mother, my relationship with Derrick, and the overall chaotic state of my life. Finally, I'd fallen asleep, but now I was wide-awake again.

Knox looped his arm around my waist, yanking my back flush against his chest. "What's wrong?"

I twisted in his arms so I could see his face. His jaw was shadowed with stubble. His eyes were heavy-lidded, yet beaming with love. His lips were soft, almost gentle looking. And at that moment, it hit me with the weight of a ton of bricks. I was meant to be with Knox. That explained the instant attraction. If I didn't know better, I'd think my mother had put Knox in my path to take care of me during this time.

"I'm just thinking about my mother. It kills me that I've spent the last fourteen years being mad at her for abandoning me."

"It's not your fault."

"I know." I leaned into him, inhaling his spicy scent. "Did I tell you how lucky I am to have found you?"

His gaze focused on my lips, his hand slid up my waist, curving around the back of my neck and his warm mouth grazed mine, sliding dreamily back and forth, turning me into knots within seconds.

"I'm the lucky one," he murmured against my mouth before deepening the kiss. His tongue breached the seam of my lips, moving against mine. I pushed him onto his back and straddled him.

His fingers slipped under my shirt, caging me with his strong arms, and my breath shortened. "You need to sleep."

I raked my teeth over my lower lip. "I need you more."

Shaking his head, he tucked a strand of hair

behind my ear. "Not now. Tell me more about your mom."

I cocked my head to the side. "What do you want to know?"

"What's your favorite memory of her?"

I rolled off him on to my side, bracing my head in my hand. "She took me to see The Nutcracker every year. I think I already told you that."

He nodded, his lips curling up at the corners. "Yeah, I remember."

"Well, so anyway, until I was eight years old, we floated around a lot." Warmth radiated through my chest as I recalled her bright smile and tinkling laugh. She was so beautiful. I couldn't believe she was dead. "Sometimes we lived in a big city and sometimes we lived in a tiny town, and The Nutcracker would be some low-budget, no-name production in a school gym. When I turned six, she promised me we'd go to New York City that year. All year, I did favors for neighbors, and we collected our spare coins in a jar. Then she told me we couldn't go because her car broke down and she used the money for repairs. We ended up at some free show of The Nutcracker put on by three- and four-year-olds."

"What happened?"

"Obviously, I was a little upset," I confirmed.

He cocked an eyebrow. "Just a little?"

I snorted. "I threw a tantrum in the parking lot and pouted the entire ride home."

He grinned. "I can see you in the back seat, arms crossed, and your nose in the air. I bet you were a cute kid."

I smiled back. "Not so much. My freckles were much more noticeable back then, and my mom dressed me in clothes two sizes too big hoping they'd last longer."

He tapped me on the tip of my nose. "Still cute."

I rolled my eyes, but it didn't stop my insides from warming. "When we got home, I ran to my room, intending to lock her out, but when I opened the door, there was the most beautiful sugar plum fairy costume on my bed with matching ballet shoes."

"What happened?"

"I put it on, of course, and we stayed up until the middle of the night baking gingerbread cookies. It was the best Christmas Eve ever." I yawned. "It's weird—looking back, I can't believe how young she was. She had me when she was nineteen."

He brushed his lips across mine. "Are you tired?"

I nodded. "Yeah. Thanks for asking about her. It helps to remember the good times. I tried to push all of that out of my mind so I didn't miss her so much."

"Glad I could help." He pulled me into his arms. "Close your eyes and try to sleep. We have a long day tomorrow."

CHAPTER THIRTY-SEVEN

Knox

It seemed like I had only drifted off to sleep five minutes earlier when something woke me. The hair on my arms lifted and my ears zeroed in on the noises inside Trinity's townhome. A soft click sounded somewhere in the distance. It could've been the icemaker or the furnace, but something told me it was much more than that. We weren't alone.

The floorboards creaked, and Trinity squeezed my hand. "What was that?"

I shook my head and held my finger to her lips, my arm rustling against the sheet. With practiced ease, I slipped out of the bed and grabbed the switchblade inside the pocket of my pants. Unfortunately, I didn't bring my gun. I knew Trinity had one, so I didn't bother. I should've put it on the nightstand before we fell asleep, but I forgot.

I reached the door to the bedroom and cracked it open without a betraying squeak of the hinges or click of the door handle. The cool air wrapped around my chest from the hallway. My gaze shifted through the shadows, finally landing on a darkened silhouette pressed against the wall.

I glanced over my shoulder at Trinity. She sat with her back pressed against the headboard, clutching the sheets against her chest. I pointed to her and then to my feet, hoping she understood I wanted her to come stand next to me. I didn't know what kind of weapons this person had, but Trinity would be a sitting duck in the bed.

Without vacillating, she slipped out of bed and tiptoed across the floor, stopping only when her front pressed against my back. Her warm exhalations whispered along my skin.

"Someone's here," she mumbled.

I nodded and pulled our bodies flush against the drywall, waiting for the person to move to the bedroom. After a minute that felt like an hour, I sensed someone just outside the door. My muscles tensed, prepared to strike, disarm, and kill if necessary. I hadn't killed anyone since I left the military. I never liked that part of my job. As a Naval Intelligence officer, it didn't happen as often as someone on the front lines, but I had killed people to protect and defend others and myself.

The door floated open, almost in slow motion, and a person dressed in black tentatively stepped over the threshold. I lunged forward, wrapping my arms around the person's shockingly small waist. We hit the ground with a loud thud.

The intruder kicked, bucked, and hit. I straddled the person's waist and immobilized his arms above his face. Trinity flipped on the overhead light, bathing the room in a yellow glow and I froze. It wasn't a man. It was a woman. Even in a dark wig, I knew it was Darcey Benton. She had icy blue eyes, a long angular nose, and sharp cheekbones. I'd never talked to her, but our paths had crossed many times since I started investigating Derrick Benton.

My muscles tensed. "Why are you here?"

Her eyes narrowed. "Get off of me. I just wanted to have a little conversation with Trinity Jones."

"I don't think so." I kept her arms pinned to the ground with one hand as I searched her for weapons. I didn't find anything except a syringe filled with clear liquid. I pulled it out of the pocket of her black wool jacket.

I waved it in front of her face. "What's this?"

She pursed her lips together, and hundreds of tiny wrinkles burst from the skin around her mouth. "It's nothing."

I held it out, and Trinity scooped it out of my hand, placing it on top of the dresser.

"Trinity," I said, keeping my eyes glued on Darcey Benton. "Grab my phone from the pocket of my pants and call Ben Livingston."

She crouched on the floor and stuffed her hand into the pocket of my discarded pants. "Who's that?"

"My contact at the FBI."

"No." Darcey Benton shook her head back and forth, strands of hair from her black wig sticking to her face. "Just hear me out. I want talk to Miss

Jones about solving this mess amicably without involving the press or anyone."

"Let her go, Knox," she said, her voice lacking emotion. "I want to hear what she has to say."

I relaxed my hands around her wrist, but I didn't move off her yet. "I think you're making a mistake. Wait until you have the benefit of your attorney's counsel tomorrow. You can't trust her."

***

Trinity

"I know that," I answered with growing numbness as I stared into Darcey Benton's icy blue eyes.

In truth, it didn't matter what she said, tonight or tomorrow. I was done with my life being stuck in neutral while I followed the Bentons' rules. I might not want my half of the trust, but I didn't think Derrick or his mother should get the money either. They didn't deserve it. With my back to Darcey and Knox, I propped his phone against a book and pressed the red button on the video camera of his phone. I spun around and used my body to shield the red light from Darcey and Knox.

"Go ahead." I planted my hands on my hips. "I don't have all night. I have an early morning appointment with my attorney."

Knox stood and Darcey climbed to her feet, brushing the invisible dirt from her long jacket.

"Your share of the trust is worth roughly fifteen million dollars. However, the terms of the trust restrain your ability to access the money. You are entitled to a small yearly allowance starting at the age of twenty-five and continuing for the remainder of your life. If you don't have children, the money will revert to Derrick or his heirs when you die."

I cocked an eyebrow. "So what's your point?"

"If you agree to sign papers giving up any right to the Benton Family Trust, and you publically deny Richard Benton was your biological father, I'm prepared to wire seven and a half million dollars into your bank account immediately."

"You want me to settle for half of the money?" I shrugged. "Why would I do that?"

She took a step forward, shrinking the gap between us. "Because you'll get all the money now and you can do whatever you want with it. You can spend it however you wish, whenever you wish."

"Hm." I leaned my hip against the dresser, pretending to consider her offer. "What do you think, Knox?"

His jaw was clamped tight. His eyes were hard. His body vibrated with anger. "That we should call the police and report a break in. I'm sure whatever is in that syringe is sufficient to charge her with attempted murder."

She curled her hands into balls and the corner of her jaw twitched. "What he thinks is irrelevant. This is between us."

"And when would I have to decide?"

"You have until seven in the morning to give me an answer. My attorney will have the documents ready to sign by ten a.m., but you have to fire your attorney. I want as little people involved as possible."

"Wow. What a bargain," I mocked. "Will the agreement give you the remainder of my half of the trust?"

"I'll split the remainder between Derrick and me. We're the only other beneficiaries."

I chuckled cynically. "That'd be quite a windfall for you."

She lifted her chin. "Seven and a half million dollars doesn't make much difference for someone like me. I have more than enough to live comfortably for the rest of my life."

"I'm not sure what I think is more entertaining." I smiled without showing any teeth. "That you're deluded enough to think I'd actually believe a word out of your mouth, or that you think I'm dumb enough to accept your offer."

Her gaze flitted to the side. "I don't have any motive to lie."

"Really?" I scoffed. "Because according to my attorney, he estimated my share of the trust to be around a hundred million dollars. He also said you have a yearly allowance with the remainder going to Derrick and me." Her face turned red, but I kept going. "So thank you for the offer. It was entertaining to listen to your lies, but I don't need until morning to tell you to fuck off."

I pointed my finger at her. "I plan to go after the entire share and more if I can get my hands on it. In fact, I won't stop until you spend your final days completely destitute. You're a liar, and I have the feeling you're a murderer, too. You killed my mom when she asked for money to support me, didn't you? You killed my cat. You trashed my townhome and threatened me."

"You can't prove it," she sneered. "Nobody will believe a trashy nobody over me."

I lifted up Knox's phone and flashed the screen. "I think I've got all I need here."

"No," she yelled, her face contorting.

In one fluid motion, she lunged forward, grabbed the syringe from the dresser and flicked off the plastic lid. With her eyes narrowed and her lips twisted, she held it over her head like a warrior with a battle axe. My hand clamped around her wrist, pushing her arm away from me. Our eyes locked. Our arms moved forward and backward. My fingernails dug into her flesh like talons.

Grunts and groans filled the air. I lowered my shoulder and rammed it into the center of her chest. Her body slammed into the dresser, and a giant puff of air exploded from her mouth.

"You bitch," she roared through clenched teeth.

She kicked the side of my leg and my knee buckled, giving her a split second advantage. She inched the syringe within striking distance of my neck, and I felt the tip drag along my skin.

I opened my mouth to scream for Knox, but he was already there. His hand wrapped around mine, and he shoved the syringe away from me, plunging it in the side of Darcey Benton's neck.

Her eyes flared and a scream erupted from her mouth. Within seconds, she collapsed to the floor, her hands clutching her heart.

Knox crouched in front of her body and pressed his fingers just below the needle lodged in her neck.

"There's nothing we can do for her," he said unnecessarily.

My vision swayed, and I collapsed on the end of the bed, dropping my head into my hands. Guilt sliced through my chest and I couldn't breathe. "Oh my God," I wheezed between gasps. "What did I do?"

"We did what we had to," he said gently. "There was no way in hell I'd let that woman hurt you."

"What now?" I mumbled between rolling sobs. My body shook from head to toe. She was evil, but I'd never hurt anyone before. With every drawn out tremor, I felt like I was coming apart at the seams.

I just helped kill someone.

Darcey Benton is dead because of me.

This isn't happening.

I can't breathe.

I'm going to be sick.

He pried my hands away from my face and kissed the top of my head. "We're going to call the police, my contact at the FBI, and your attorney."

My stomach rolled for the hundredth time as I gaped at Darcey Benton's lifeless body. Her eyes stared sightlessly at the ceiling. Her mouth was lax and her hands were curled around the lapels of her jacket. I couldn't believe this woman intended to kill me over money.

"What are we going to say?" My voice sounded as if I had swallowed a cup of glass.

"We're going to tell the truth. We don't have anything to hide." He managed a faint smile. "And, thanks to you, we have the video to support our story."

"Yes, we do," I said softly, my muscles unknotting a tiny bit. I wrapped my arms around his neck, tears burning the corners of my eyes. His arms circled my waist, and he rocked me back and forth. Just being in his arms quieted my fears. I trusted him to guide me through this because nothing seemed insurmountable with him by my side. "I love you. I should've told you earlier, but I was too afraid that you'd reject me. Then I acted like a jerk the other night and I'll understand if you're done with me. I don't expect you to say anything back or profess your undying love. I just wanted—"

"Shut up, Jones." He pressed two fingers to my lips and shook his head. "If I didn't love you, I would've dumped you weeks ago. I was just waiting for the right time to tell you."

I leaned back, smirking. "Is that your way of telling me you love me and you can't live without me?"

"Yes. I guess it was," he said with a playful grin.

"Well, I would've hoped for a more romantic setting, but I'll give you a pass given the circumstances." I cocked my head toward Darcey Benton. "We should do something about her."

"Yeah, we should." His eyes met mine for an endless moment. "But first I want to hold you for a while and make sure you're okay."

I nodded because there was no need for words. I was alive, and Knox loved me. After decades of living in the shadows of the Benton family's sins and lies, being with him was all that mattered.

EPILOGUE

Knox

Two months later…

I pulled through the gates of Archer's home in L.A. and cut the engine. The full moon peeked through the swaying palm trees lining the front walkway to the large white Mediterranean home with its rust-colored barrel tiled roof. Iron lanterns strategically placed next to the arched front door winked at us in invitation.

I glanced at Trinity in the passenger seat next to me, and a feeling of ease and overwhelming happiness swept through me, as if all of the wrongs fate had committed against my brother and me had finally been righted. Archer found the love of his life in Langley and mine was sitting right next to me.

After his mother's death, Derrick Benton quickly and quietly settled all matters pertaining to Trinity's share of the Benton Family Trust. In exchange, Trinity agreed not to contest Derrick's public statement that his mother had a heart attack.

Since the night Darcey Benton showed up at Trinity's house, she had refused to have any contact with her half-brother. Instead, she funneled all conversations through her attorney. I didn't know how long her determination to stay away from him would continue. Now that he had renounced his bid for reelection, he had plenty of time on his hands, and he made weekly attempts to heal the divide. I didn't want him in our lives, but it was Trinity's choice, and I'd support her either way.

Miles Knightly turned himself in to the FBI a month and a half ago. In exchange for immunity, he agreed to help prosecutors mount a case against Dima Antonov for the blackmail scheme involving Lang and Benton. Miles collapsed and died in his home two weeks ago. The police were still struggling to establish the cause of his death, but the FBI suspected Antonov had something to do with it.

"Are you ready to go inside?" I asked.

She twirled the diamond solitaire on her finger. "As ready as ever."

I tapped her ring. "How long before one of them notices the ring?

I proposed to Trinity last week. I'd spent my entire life avoiding commitment, but it didn't take me long to realize I wanted to spend my life with her. When she agreed to marry me, I asked her if she had a date in mind. She said as soon as possible. We were married the next day.

She smiled, holding out her hand. The diamond shot rainbows of light across the dashboard. "Langley will notice within five minutes."

"You're probably right. After we go in, there's

no turning back. You'll be stuck with me forever."

"I already thought I was."

"I like the way you think."

I brushed my lips across hers, then bit her lower lip teasingly. When she opened her mouth to mine, I couldn't stop myself. I pulled her across the console and slipped my hands underneath her short black skirt. I closed my eyes as her lips explored a path down my neck.

Bang.

Bang.

Bang.

"Are you guys coming inside or what?" Archer said, smirking.

I rolled down the window. "Go away. Can't you see we're busy?"

"Yeah, well, I don't care. You can continue this later. You're already an hour late and Gunnar has been here for at least thirty minutes." Archer shook his head. "I need you to run interference."

"Yeah. Yeah. Give me another minute," I said, sliding Trinity off my lap.

Trinity pushed her long dark hair behind her ears. "Who's Gunnar?"

I watched Archer make his way back inside his house. "My other brother."

Her brows scrunched together. "Wait. You never told me about another brother. What's wrong with him?"

I closed my eyes for a second, remembering my little brother. We never really clicked. After his paternal grandparents won custody of him, his life was so different from Archer's and mine. He had the world at his fingertips, whereas Archer and I still wallowed in the hell created by our mom without an end in sight. It'd been ten years since I'd seen him. He probably wasn't so little anymore.

"You'll see. He's a man of few words."

"Should I be nervous?"

"No. He's harmless." I squeezed her hand, and cracked open the car door. "Let's do this so we can make our excuses and start our honeymoon."

She glanced at her phone. "Ten hours and counting until our flight. Do you think you can wait that long?"

I took her hand in mine, our future stretching out before us, and not for the first time since I had met Trinity Jones, I couldn't believe my luck. "I'd wait for you forever."

Facebook:
https://www.facebook.com/lcardiff11

Twitter:
https://twitter.com/lcardiff_author

Website:
http://lisacardiff.com/

Goodreads:
https://www.goodreads.com/author/show/7692079.
Lisa_Cardiff

9 781680 584912